MY HEARTBEAT

MY HEARTBEAT

Garret Freymann-Weyr

HOUGHTON MIFFLIN COMPANY
Boston 2002

www.houghtonmifflinbooks.com

The text of this book is set in Janson and Altemus Cuts.

Library of Congress Cataloging-in-Publication Data

Weyr, Garret.
    My heartbeat / Garret Freymann-Weyr.
        p. cm.
    Summary: As she tries to understand the closeness between her older brother and his best friend, fourteen-year-old Ellen finds her relationship with each of them changing.
        ISBN 0-618-14181-2
    [1. Brothers and sisters—Fiction. 2. Homosexuality—Fiction. 3. Interpersonal relations—Fiction. 4. Family life—Fiction.]

PZ7.W5395 My 2002
[Fic]—dc21

                                                          2001047059

Manufactured in the United States of America
QUM 10 9 8 7 6 5 4 3 2 1

*To Papa, for the years of attention,
and Jeff, for the room with a door*

CHAPTER ONE

IT'S AFTER MIDNIGHT WHEN I HEAR JAMES LEAVE. THE summer house in Maine is old and full of misleading noises, but it is his leaving that I hear. Since I am listening for it, I wonder if it counts as eavesdropping. I get out of bed and cross to the front window. I see James walk down the path, open the gate, and turn right. Toward town. Without my brother.

Link probably heard James leave as well. My brother knows better than I why his best friend has gone off alone. I spend a lot of time with the two of them, but I wouldn't say I know them. Not in a complete way. They have their own secrets, if that's the right word. It's more that sometimes Link is unhappy with James or vice versa and I don't know why. Mom says it's normal for best friends not to get along sometimes.

"Everyone in the world has a different way of looking at the same thing," she says.

They certainly look different, which I only noticed early last year. After constantly thinking of him as an extension of my brother, one day I looked at James and thought, *He has the best face*. It is full of long eyelashes and hidden smiles. Link's face is neither mysterious or beautiful.

A few days after I first noticed this difference between them, Link asked me why I was turning red every time James came over. I spent weeks dodging his question, before finally blurting out that I thought James was super cute. I was only in the seventh grade, so *super cute* was the best cover I could come up with for *totally madly in love*.

Of course, Link told James, who went out of his way to say how very flattered he was. "When you grow out of it, you will break my heart," he said. Almost two years later, I'm still *totally madly in love* with James, but I'm more used to it. He and Link try teasing me about it. They get into a contest to see which one of them can make me blush. It's more boring for them now that I don't turn red every time I see James, but I do like his face and hope he will like mine someday.

Until then, he is my brother's to understand, and together they are the people I enjoy most in the world. Except when they are unhappy with each other. That might not be the case tonight, but it's really unusual for one of them to go out without the other. Also, they had a kind of fight last night, which could still be brewing. It was totally weird and totally typical.

We were watching a movie that James had rented. Mom and Dad had already gone to bed. The movie was in Swedish, which was no surprise. Almost every movie Link and James make me sit through has subtitles. This one, at least, was in color, but there were so many dream sequences that the plot was impossible to follow. About an hour into it, Link said, "We've seen this. Last year at Film Forum."

"I know," James said.

"We didn't think it was so great then," Link said.

"I didn't like it," James said. "You did."

"Not enough to sit through it again," Link said, and I watched James's face in the pale light that the video (now on "pause") gave off. "Why are we watching this?"

"I want to double-check my opinion," James said.

"For whose benefit?" Link asked, his voice suddenly tight and harsh, like when he is telling Mom that whatever she's asking is none of her business.

"Whose do you think," James said more than asked.

"You're kidding," my brother said. "We're watching four hours of Bergman on account of that guy?"

"He's in the cinema studies department," James said.

"At Penn State," Link said. "Not exactly the place to get your degree in cinema studies from."

They will both be seniors in high school this fall, and they have been researching colleges and universities all summer. Link wants to go to MIT or Stanford, and James wants to go to Brown or Stanford. Mom says they can both be unbearably arrogant about where people go to school. Dad, who went to Yale and is dying for Link to go there, says they have good standards and not to discourage them.

"There are people for whom one chooses to make exceptions," James said, and I froze, shifting my gaze to my brother.

I am pretty sure they were talking about one of the waiters at Cooper's Terrace, which is a café on the other side of the island. They've hung out with him, even though I don't think either of them likes him. They say he plays tennis really well, and the way they say it is like an insult. It's always bad when they have different opinions about the same person. So if James were suddenly to like the waiter whom he and Link have been insulting ever since we got here, it would be bad.

"And you think he's one of those people," Link said. "How interesting of you."

"It's not that interesting," James said, hitting the "stop" button on the remote. "And the movie is exactly the way I remember it. We don't have to finish."

"Oh, no, please," Link said, standing up. "Don't let my opinions come between you and the tennis champion with his degree from nowhere."

And he was gone. Out of the room and up the stairs.

"Your brother," James said, the way he always does

when he wants me to understand that Link is being unreasonable for no reason.

"You'd better get him," I said, the way I always do when Link stomps out of the room. Which is often. My whole family's reaction to any kind of conflict is to avoid it. Each of us would prefer to spend money or chew off a limb rather than have a fight. Our aversion to fights is a quiet one except for Link. He always makes a big drama out of removing himself from an argument. The rest of us are more low-key about it.

"Do you ever tell him to get me?" James asked.

"You don't stomp out as often," I said. "Besides, Link never listens to me."

"He should," James said. "You're the smart one in the family."

"Sure," I said.

Link skipped third grade because he could already do long division and fractions in his head. He taught himself to read. I am not an idiot, but I am not the smart one in the family.

"I'd better go beg him to listen to me," James said, and he went upstairs.

By the time they both came back down, I'd fallen asleep on the couch, and, after they'd woken me up, we decided that our Swedish film festival was done. They seemed cheerful with each other today, full of plans and secrets for my birthday. I will be fourteen tomorrow. If James and Link are still in a fight, my birthday will be ruined. I decide to go knock on Link's door and tell him I can't sleep.

When I was little we used to sleep in each other's rooms the night before all special occasions: Christmas, trips to Europe, first days of school, and birthdays. We stopped when I was nine or ten. I don't remember which one of us decided we were too old or if anything was said. It just stopped. Special occasions now come and go without our marking it by sleeping in the same room. Link's not exactly Mr. Hospitality tonight, saying, in response to my knock, "I told you no."

"It's Ellen," I say, knowing he hasn't told me no in a few days.

"It's open for you," he says and I go in.

"Who'd you tell no?" I ask, settling carefully into the broken armchair near his bed.

"Your mother," he says.

When he's mad at Mom or Dad, they become *your mother* or *your father*, as if I were responsible for their behavior. It's my policy never to ask why he's mad at them. Why borrow trouble?

"James went out," I say.

"Yeah, I know," Link says. "Your mother wanted to know where he went."

"Do you know?" I ask.

"Ellen, it's late."

"I don't think he likes that guy at all," I say, wanting to reassure him. And probably myself.

"Which guy?" Link asks, sitting up in bed. "What are you talking about?"

"The tennis champion," I say.

"Oh, that. He was just kidding, Ellen. You can't take James seriously."

"So where is he?" I ask.

"I don't know," Link says. "He wanted to go out and I didn't. End of story."

"How come?"

"How come what?" Link asks.

I don't say anything. He's not asking me a question so much as telling me it's none of my business. He never says that to me in a flat-out way, of course. It's more Link's style to put all the important information into what he doesn't say. Sometimes I understand him and lots of times I don't. Tonight I do.

"He should have asked you to go," Link says. "You would have gone with him."

"I might," I say. Probably. Sure. No doubt about it.

"You would," my brother says. "You would follow James to the moon."

I don't say anything, and after a while Link asks if I want to sleep in his room.

"Yes," I say. "Because it's my birthday tomorrow."

"It's two in the morning," Link says. "Tomorrow is here."

He gets out of bed, and while he's whispering (instead of singing) "Happy Birthday," he clears a space on the floor, where he makes up a sleeping area with a quilt and two of his pillows.

"You take the bed," he says, the way he used to when I was nine.

I lie awake for a long time. For hours after Link has drifted off to sleep. I listen for and I hear James returning to the house. It is true I would follow James to the moon. But if Link would let me, I would follow him anywhere he wanted.

CHAPTER TWO

THERE IS A CAKE AND TWO DIFFERENT KINDS OF ice cream. Dad made the cake and cut it into the shape of a Saint Bernard. I love dogs. Big dogs. The kind of dogs who would be hideously unhappy living in New York City. There are fourteen candles crammed into the Saint Bernard's ear. I'm not sure I have a wish worth fourteen candles, so I just blow them out and watch the smoke drift lazily up. Then I open my presents.

Link gives me a pair of Rollerblades, which I have wanted since two summers ago. I know that James has to have helped pay for these, but that it was Link who got Mom finally to agree that I could have a pair. Mom gives me a helmet along with elbow and knee pads.

"If you don't wear the helmet, Mom will personally kill us," Link says.

James hands me an envelope. Inside it are two bumper stickers. One says Visualize Whirled Peas, which is a goofy way of saying Visualize World Peace. The other one says I Haven't Been the Same Since That House Fell on My Sister.

"Whose sister?" I ask.

James reminds me about *The Wizard of Oz* and how Dorothy's house kills the Wicked Witch of the West's sister.

"It's a joke," he says.

And it is funny even if it has to be explained.

"Very campy," Mom says.

"I told him not to pick that one," Link says.

I like it, but I mostly make a big effort never to agree with James against my brother. And vice versa.

"I would love to put this on the car," Mom says.

"No," Dad says firmly. "No."

"I don't have a car," I say, sounding as stupid as I feel. What am I supposed to do with a bumper sticker? Not to mention one that Mom likes but Link doesn't.

"They're for your helmet," James says. "So it won't look geeky."

"Not that there's anything wrong with geeky," Link says before Dad has a chance to. *Geeky* is one of Dad's favorite words, and I listen with glee to my brother's imitation of our father: "Geeky people often have that which is most valuable in this life." Link pauses here for effect, so that James and I can join in, shouting Dad's favorite phrase, "A mind with its own heartbeat!"

Dad laughs. It makes him feel appreciated when Link makes fun of him. Dad's present is a hardcover copy of *The Age of Innocence*. It's by Edith Wharton, who also wrote *Ethan Frome*, which I have been trying to read all summer. It is required reading for incoming ninth graders at Cedar Hill, where I will start school in two weeks. I have read the first thirteen pages of *Ethan Frome* five times. It is boring beyond belief. Dad says if I have to read a book by Edith Wharton, then *The Age of Innocence* is the one to read.

"I didn't read it until last year," Link says. "Ellen's too young."

"Girls mature faster," Dad says.

I look at Link in what I hope is a mature way, and he crosses his eyes and sticks his tongue out. I laugh. James smiles one of his hidden smiles, which only come out for Link.

"Neither of you is at all mature," James says.

"Like you can tell," Link says.

"I am older and wiser," James says, and Link laughs with disbelief. James, who did not skip third grade, is a year older than Link. Sometimes they fight about this year between them as if it were a bridge too short to close their private gap.

It's pouring rain, which happens more often than not in Maine, so there's no chance to try out my Rollerblades. Instead, I spend the afternoon and half the night reading my new book. I am probably missing the whole point, but I think it's a love story. The man's name is Newland

Archer. I keep picturing James, though. Probably because Newland is in love with a woman named the Countess Ellen Olenska.

I never thought my name could sound as wonderful as that. Every minute that I am reading, I *am* the Countess Ellen Olenska. And Newland/James is in love with me. Really in love with me, as opposed to the kind that only happens in my head.

The next morning it is still raining. Link has gone running by the time I drag myself out of bed. He is on the track team at school and runs, rain or shine, seven miles every other day. James says that the running is the only part of my brother he cannot—will not—approve of. James has asthma, and his opinion of anything athletic is fairly low. He says running is a total waste of Link's time. I privately think it's kind of cool that Link has something he does no matter what. He won't even eat sweets because, he says, sugar makes him slow.

I love sweets, and I have a huge piece of leftover birthday cake for breakfast because there is no one around to stop me. Dad is locked up in the dining room, doing work. He has a strategy meeting the day after we get back and has spent most of the month preparing for it. Mom and James are playing backgammon in the living room while I sit in the kitchen, reading and getting cake crumbs all over the place.

It rains all day, and I read eighty-five pages until I think my head will burst. I get so mixed up with James as Newland and me as the Countess that it's hard to understand a lot of the book. Newland is engaged to someone who is not the Countess, and the Countess is in some kind of social disgrace. It's not clear what, because no one will say anything about her. There are just a lot of hints and averted looks. I don't know how Newland is going to break his engagement or how they'll clear up the Countess's messy social situation, but I keep reading.

At dinner, which is takeout pizza because Dad was too busy to cook, I have trouble looking at James without thinking of myself as a countess. It's kind of nice to be a countess instead of a girl scarfing down pizza. So I keep looking at James, sitting up straight, and imagining that I am at a dinner party with footmen serving iced melons and lots of wine. Dad, who does not approve of daydreaming, tells me to stop staring at James.

"I'm not," I say, sitting up even straighter.

"You are," Link says.

"She's not staring at me," James says.

"She is totally staring at you," Link says.

"Leave her in peace," James says.

I resolve to finish *Age of Innocence* as soon as possible so as to avoid any further character confusion. The weather cooperates with my plan by being super foggy in the morning. At least the rain has stopped, but the air is so humid no one has the energy to go anywhere. James and Link are reading *A Tale of Two Cities* and are racing to see who will finish first. James will win because he skips any part of a book that bores him, whereas Link is devoted to each page.

13

I am far enough along in my book to realize that this isn't going to be a love story where the lovers wind up together. Neither Newland or the Countess can bring themselves to say the obvious: I love you and no one else. Newland, in particular, is so concerned with what people might think of him that when he sends the Countess flowers, he doesn't include a card. The Countess doesn't want to upset anyone and therefore never asks for anything. Not even the thing she wants most, which is for Newland to love her. This seems like an unbelievably horrible way to live your life. I guess I'm glad I'm not a countess after all. By three in the afternoon, James is seventy pages ahead of Link and dying to get out of the house.

"Let's take Ellen," Link says. "She stopped reading an hour ago."

James, who has his driver's license, gets Mom to loan him her car. We go to Cooper's Terrace, which would make me incredibly tense except that it was Link's choice. I don't see their tennis-playing waiter anywhere, so that's a relief. We sit inside, and they order iced tea with mint and lemon. I get chocolate layer cake and refuse to share it with James, who says he only wants one bite. I've seen many a dessert disappear completely under James's one-bite policy.

While I'm eating, Link goes to the piano in the music alcove and starts to play. He hasn't studied piano in years because he didn't practice seriously enough when he had lessons. Dad said it was a waste of time and talent. Maybe so, but Link can play almost anything by ear. James plays the piano really well (Link says his technique is excellent), but he needs to have sheet music in front of him. James thinks his own piano lessons are boring, but he loves when Link plays. They listen to a lot of music together to see if Link will be able to play it after hearing it just once.

Sometimes, when he is at a piano, Link will play a song for me. Dumb songs that I love from *The Sound of Music* and *Camelot*. I never request anything, of course. I think half the reason the two of them let me spend so much time in their company is that they forget I'm there. It's why I have to hide just how much I am *totally madly in love* with James. It makes them notice me. And that makes them more careful around me, which is not what I want.

In fact, if I'd made a birthday wish, it would have been to hear them when James begs Link to listen to him. To know more about their different ways of looking at the same things. Be it a movie, a college, or a person. To understand better why they waste time reminding each other that they don't always agree. I make the wish now, with no singing or candles to blow out. Just some crumbs of cake and melted ice cubes to look at.

It's enough.

CHAPTER THREE

I FINISH READING MY BOOK THE DAY WE LEAVE FOR home. I liked it, although I was right about the ending. Newland never got to marry the Countess. Just loved her without doing anything about it. It was sad but pretty.

The endless drive home is made even longer because of a horrible traffic jam crossing into New Hampshire. When we finally get home, it takes forever to unpack the car. I can never believe how much stuff we take with us to Maine. It's ridiculous. Link says we travel like refugees, but James says refugees don't have time to pack. Either way, it's a long time before the car is ready to go to the garage. Mom offers to drop James off at home, but he says his parents are away until tomorrow. Does she mind if he stays over?

"What do you mean, 'away'?" Mom asks James.

Turns out that Mr. and Mrs. Wentworth decided to go to Canada for two weeks, since they wouldn't have to worry about entertaining James. That's exactly how he puts it.

"They were really grateful to you guys," James says. "They wouldn't have had a vacation otherwise. They don't like to do things when they have to worry about entertaining me."

James's parents are lawyers at a firm on Wall Street. They work even more than Mom and Dad do, but not because they need the money. Mr. Wentworth is from one of those families that haven't spent the whole trust fund yet. Mom says Mr. and Mrs. Wentworth are not qualified to be people, let alone fit to be parents. Dad says they are probably good lawyers and Mom shouldn't badmouth James's parents in front of him. So this evening she says only that James is all the entertainment she could ever want.

Normally she'd make up the sofa bed in Dad's study, but Dad will be up all night getting his presentation ready. I will sleep on the scratchy couch in the living room so that James can have my room. No matter where we are, Link and James get their own space. Dad says that boys need a lot of privacy, and Mom says, be that as it may, she wouldn't inflict any of our guest beds on a guest. I am always happy to vacate my room for James.

After dinner, Dad vanishes into his study. I do the dishes while Mom starts putting together proposals for her fall projects. She's an interior designer, and she never knows just how crazy her schedule will be. The TV and VCR are in the living room, which means I stay up late. I am partly watching a movie in Cantonese and partly listening to James and Link discuss which movie by John Woo is the best ever. If school weren't going to start in a week, I'd be totally happy that we're home.

We begin every September determined to continue our summer habit of having a civilized sit-down dinner during which we each review our day and discuss future plans. Mom likes to say the McConnell family dinner hour is sacred. And it is. I like hearing how everyone is and what Mom is working on or if Link has a track meet or Dad a plane to catch. It's nice, although, truth be told, our sacred hour tends to erode as the year progresses. The night before school starts, dinner is in full force.

Dad's strategy meeting went well, but he's going to have to travel more than he'd like. The company he works for wants to open five new hotels in five different cities over the next three years. It's going to involve a lot of planning for many different, uniquely important meetings. Mom has put design proposals in at the Locust Club, two medical offices in Brooklyn Heights, and one private home on Long Island. Dad asks Link if he has reenrolled at his math program up at Columbia. It's for kids in high school who are doing college-level math.

"Yes," Link says. "I have already arranged to sacrifice my Saturdays at the altar of higher education."

"You don't have to do it," Mom says. "Remember it's your choice."

"He wants to do it," Dad says. "Link lives for math."

"I said it was Link's choice," Mom says to Dad.

When Link was in the seventh grade, Dad wanted to send him to a boarding school in New Hampshire where he could do nothing but math. Mom said Link was way too young to make that kind of a commitment, and Link himself didn't want to leave home. Dad said that if Mom would just agree with him about New Hampshire, they could persuade Link to go. Mom actually wound up screaming at Dad.

I don't remember what she said, just that she screamed and that in response Dad said, very quietly, that he was disappointed in her. I was only in the fourth grade, but Link, who remembers the whole thing, says our parents almost got divorced. Instead, Dad gave up on boarding school, but he and Mom still have different ideas about Link's life.

"I want to," Link says to Mom now. "It's a good program."

"There you are," Dad says and then asks me how I am enjoying *The Age of Innocence*.

"She's done," Link says. "She finished reading it in Maine."

"What did you think?"

The thing about Dad is that he makes you want and dread his attention at the same time. I like the fact that he's interested in my thoughts, but I'm always terrified of

19

what he thinks about what I think. After all, I know he's judging whether or not my mind has any kind of a heartbeat yet. What can I safely say about what I thought?

"It was good," I say. "But I wish there had been a happy ending."

"It's hard to find a happy ending in a good book," Dad says.

"What, only bad books have happy endings?" Link asks.

"You're simplifying," Dad says to him, and to me he says, "A good book is a reflection of some kind of truth."

Talking with Dad can go two ways. One, he knows you don't understand what he's talking about and he is disappointed in you. Two, he doesn't know and so keeps on talking, which gives you a chance to figure it out. In the hope of arriving at the second way, I don't ask what reflecting truth has to do with books.

"Happy endings, while desirable, aren't always true," Dad says.

Except, of course, for the ones that are. Right? I don't ask.

"I don't care so much about a true ending," I say instead. "I'd like a happy one next time. That's all."

Dad says he'll see what he can do. Link is out the door as soon as dinner is over. He and James have tickets for a play on Broadway. It's a revival of some big, serious play from England. The entire run is sold out. One of Mr. Wentworth's clients gave the tickets to him, and he gave them to James. If Mr. Wentworth has any free time, he plays squash or goes out to dinner with Mrs. Wentworth. Link and James get a lot of tickets to plays and concerts in this way.

I mope around the apartment, wondering how complicated and/or awful ninth grade will be. When Dad comes into my room to say good night, he has a musty-smelling paperback copy of *Pride and Prejudice*, by Jane Austen.

"I think you'll like the ending," he says.

I read in bed for an hour before falling asleep. It's very slow going and the sentences are endless.

Because I am new this year, I am due at Cedar Hill a day before James and Link, who, as returning students, don't need orientation. I, along with nineteen other new students (mostly girls), get a tour of classrooms, locker assignments, and class schedules and the chance to pick up school uniforms. They are beyond hideous. At least for the girls.

I get three green skirts, five white blouses, and two gray button-down sweaters with a Cedar Hill badge sewn on the front. The boys have it a little better. They wear khaki pants, a dress shirt, a tie, and a gray blazer with a Cedar Hill badge sewn on the front. I know from James and Link that the boys never wear their ties outside of assembly. They carry them in their pants' pocket. Blazers and sweaters alike hang in lockers, unworn throughout the year. No matter how cold it is.

We have to get weighed and measured before they can

give us our clothes. I am, as far as I can tell, the tallest girl here. And the one in the least need of a bra. Judging by today, it's clear I will never learn anyone's name. My brain has been such a sieve that I have already forgotten my locker number. This is not the fresh start I was hoping for.

I didn't exactly love my old school. Since it only went up to the eighth grade, it was a given that I would be leaving by the time I got to the ninth grade. I spent a lot of last year convincing myself that once I got to Cedar Hill, I would love school and whatever problems I had would disappear. Not that I had a ton of problems, but there were some.

I did well at school. At least, I did all my homework on time, and I never passed notes in class or shouted out an answer. But it wasn't good enough. Mom and Dad were always getting letters from my teachers and having to go in for special conferences. "Ellen exhibits," the school said, "an unwillingness to form any firm social attachments. There is a consistent failure on Ellen's part to connect with or thrive in any of the many groups which make themselves available to her."

I can tell by watching the fourteen girls in various stages of undress that I am the only one not making an effort to "form social attachments." The girls laugh, talking about how ugly the skirts are or how they must go on a diet immediately or how their summers were. My continued "consistent failure" is mostly due to the fact that I know how my summer was, I don't need a diet, and the skirts' appearance speaks for itself.

For me to go through the agonizing process of getting into a conversation with someone I don't know, it has to be worth it. One of the things I love best about my brother and James is that everything is worth it to them. They can spend an hour talking about whether or not to wear their khaki pants cuffed or hanging over the backs of their shoes. And they can make it sound as if the fate of the world depends on what they do with the hems of their pants. It's just their way.

Once I have been measured and given my quota of skirts, tops, and unusable sweaters, I retreat to a corner of the room and open *Pride and Prejudice*. The girl in it is named Elizabeth, and she has four or six sisters (I can't tell her friends apart from her sisters). All of them desperately want to get married. Their conversations are almost as boring as the ones currently surrounding me.

I know I need to make more of an effort this year if I want to stop the letters criticizing my social skills. It's a new school, and I have resolved to make a fresh start. I will smile more. A gesture of goodwill, even if I have no intention of following through to any kind of connection, firm or otherwise.

CHAPTER FOUR

My FACE HURTS FROM SMILING AT SO MANY PEOPLE I
don't know. The kids in my class are really friendly.
Everyone wants to know everything about everybody else.
It's completely terrifying, but I manage to meet everyone
without having to know anybody. The trick with school is
staying out of people's way. This works pretty well most of
the time. At my old school it was only from the grownups
that I got attention solely by trying to avoid it.

Here, however, there is a slight problem with staying
out of the way. Girls. Lots of girls. Not in my grade, but
from eleventh and twelfth and maybe a few from tenth.
One after another, these girls come up to me either in the
courtyard or by my locker (which I finally located).

"You're Ellen McConnell," they say, and I agree without elaborating. Yes, yes I am.

"So you must know James really well," most of them say, although several ask, "How close are you and Link?"

To the James group, I say, "Well enough," and to the smaller, Link group, I say, "Close enough."

A big part of staying out of the way is giving answers that are evasive without being memorable. Each girl tells me to tell Link or James that she says hi. I wonder why saying hi needs to go through a third party and worry I am being set up for a practical joke. When I look for my brother and/or James to deliver these messages (although there is no point, I have forgotten each girl's name), they are nowhere to be found.

On the third day of school I understand why, if you didn't live with one of them, saying hi to James or Link might be problematic. There is a break every morning after assembly. Everyone goes out into the courtyard. At first I think Link and James are never there, until I look up and see them sitting overhead on the fire escape. James, despite his asthma, is smoking. Link is going through James's sketchbook.

James wants to be an artist and Link is his critic. Although I have never been allowed to see any of James's drawings, I am allowed to watch Link look at them. I have done that a bazillion times. From down here in the courtyard I see something that I had never noticed before. Together, James and Link look like people who would be disturbed (insulted or offended is probably a better word) by anyone saying hi.

During lunch I sit with two girls from my class named Adena Cohen and Laurel Keller. Adena is new this year too, but she knows who everyone is and she is always in a good mood. Laurel is the younger sister of the first girl who asked me if Link and I were close.

"You have no idea," Laurel says. "Polly has been in love with Link since the seventh grade."

"He's the one I'd pick," Adena says.

"No, James is much cuter," Laurel says. "But Polly thinks it's too obvious he doesn't have time for girls."

I think it's just as obvious that Link's time is similarly engaged, but I don't say anything. My brother's and James's lack of time for girls isn't something I've ever thought about in quite those terms. And the terms, spoken aloud by people I don't really know, sound different from when I make quiet note of them. I don't particularly like the way they sound spoken aloud, although I don't know why. I suppose I could ask Laurel to clarify what her sister means, but I won't. I don't sit with Adena and Laurel to make conversation, but to avoid the attention that comes when you sit by yourself during lunch.

And then there is the homework attention. I have a lot of homework. Cedar Hill is a preparatory school. What can this much homework prepare you for, I'd like to know. Other than college, which had better be as amazing as James and Link make it sound. I'm going to have to work so hard to get Bs that I will probably flip over the line into straight As. This is going to put me right in the firing line of attention from teachers. My math, history, and science teachers each pull me aside to ask if it's true that I'm Lincoln McConnell's sister.

Again, I agree without elaborating. Yes, yes I am.

They rush on to say how they expect great things from me. What a joy it has been to have Link in their classes. If I have any hope of staying out of the way, a reputation as the Second Coming of Lincoln McConnell is the last thing I need. If it weren't for Dad, I'd pick two subjects to screw up deliberately. The one time I got a C by accident, he acted as if I'd been arrested for shoplifting or something.

It's not that Dad is a grown-up grade grubber, but our grades are the only objective measure he has of our education. And our education is how our minds will develop a life, never mind a heartbeat. Link says Dad wanted to be a teacher and takes out his career frustrations on us. I asked once if it were true he wanted to be a teacher, and Dad said, "No, only a linguist." Whatever that is. In any event, my father has no patience for people who don't utilize all of their talents or take advantage of all their opportunities.

Pride and Prejudice continues to be boring, and I cannot bring myself to finish it, which I know my father will call a botched opportunity to learn something. James, rejoicing in what he calls my good taste, rents the movie version so I can find out what happens without reading it. The movie's in black and white, but it has Laurence Olivier, whom I love and know from *That Hamilton Woman*. Link owns the video and watches it on nights before he races. Dad says Winston Churchill wrote the screenplay.

Twenty minutes into it, Link says *Pride and Prejudice* is unwatchable and that I'm just going to have to tell Dad that I hated the book. I tell him fine. It's not like it was my idea to watch the movie. James tells Link to go to the video store and come back with something good. As soon as Link leaves, James and I hit the kitchen for anything with sugar in it.

"How's school?" he asks.

It's good to hear the question from him. He is not asking about homework the way Dad does or about friends the way Mom does.

"Okay," I say.

"Just okay?"

"You know," I say. "It's school."

"People nice? I see you eating with those girls."

"Have to eat with someone," I say, deciding not to tell him I see him smoking. "A lot of girls like you. The first couple of days almost every girl in the school told me to tell you hi."

"Every girl?" he asks, pleasure and disbelief spreading across his face. His perfect and beautiful face.

"Not the ones in seventh and eighth grade," I say slowly, trying not to stare at him. "And some of them wanted to say hi to Link."

"Well, it's a small school, and there aren't a lot of people to say hi to."

And that's that, I think, until Link comes back and James tells him about all the undelivered messages.

"Gross," Link says. "Tell them you do not pass on greetings."

"How do you like the competition from all those girls?" James asks me. "Or have you outgrown me now that you're in high school?"

Both Link and James like for him to ask this: "Have you outgrown me?" And I always answer, "No, not yet." Tonight, I want to tease them back and I say, "What competition? I'll tell you hi to your face. Hi, James."

"Hi, James," Link says in a perfect imitation of me imitating a girl from school.

"That's enough," James says. "Let's watch the video."

Link has rented a totally gruesome war movie, which he says took millions of dollars to make. It's based on a novel by Joseph Conrad, who has not, James tells me, written anything with a happy ending. I go to bed before it's finished. There are too many helicopters.

As I anticipated, Dad is not thrilled to hear that my reading has run out of steam. When I tell him I don't like the characters in *Pride and Prejudice*, he asks why in this way that sounds like he suspects I'm lying.

"They're tense and anxious," I say. "In *The Age of Innocence* they were plain old unhappy."

I brace myself for another why, but amazingly enough Dad laughs and unearths a copy of *Jane Eyre* from the chaotic shelves in his study.

"It's romantic drivel with a happy ending," he says, "but the characters should be unhappy enough for you."

I am immediately obsessed with these characters and love them. The James character in *Jane Eyre* is named Mr. Rochester. This is the best book I have ever read. Ever. I don't know how this will have a happy ending, but it might involve a ghost. The house where Mr. Rochester lives is definitely haunted.

Eating lunch with Adena and Laurel feels like a complete waste of time. I could be reading. I try to follow their conversation, but I haven't seen the same movies they have. Worse, I don't know any of the kids in our class whom they are discussing in detail. Alarming detail. I feel a hand fall on my shoulder and turn around to face James.

"Come eat with us, Ellen," he says, pointing toward a table in the corner where he and Link eat. James picks up my tray, nodding hello to Adena and Laurel.

"Nothing against you, girls, but we need her more than you do."

I follow James to the corner table. Link moves his books aside to make space for me, explaining how James believes that if I *have* to eat with someone, it might as well be them. I pass James my cupcake without his having to ask, and he winks at me.

"No public flirting, please," Link says.

At dinner, Mom announces that she landed every job for which she submitted a proposal. Dad gets two extra wine-glasses and pours some wine for Link and me so we can be part of the toast. We all clink glasses and say, "Brava, much luck, and many more."

We're always very happy for Mom about her jobs. When she and Dad met, she was working for a catering company. Then she was a party planner. After I was born, she went back to school so she could learn to decorate.

Mom is Dad's favorite example of someone whose mind has its own heartbeat. Mom, he likes to tell us, utilizes her talents and takes full advantage of all her opportunities. Which is a good thing because living in Manhattan with two kids in private school is not cheap. Or so we are told.

"It's not that we can't afford you," Dad will say. "It's that we need to work hard in order to do so."

After the dishes are taken care of, I do homework at the kitchen table. My desk is always piled too high with books, papers, and dirty clothes for me to use. Link and Mom are the neat ones in the family. Dad and I are slobs in constant search of a clean surface. He has two desks in his study: one to work at and one to pile things on.

Mom has a small desk in the corner of the dining room. She can work on five things at once and never leave a trace. Before going to bed I stop by her desk to say good night. She hits "save" on her laptop and tells me she wants us to go clothes shopping.

"You've outgrown all your regular clothes again," she

says. "And I'm sick to death of your green skirts."

"Okay," I say. I like new clothes. The way they slide down your skin, promising to make you different. Or at least new.

I get caught reading *Jane Eyre* in French class. When Ms. Detert asks to see what has my undivided attention, I have to pass the book up four rows of desks. She glances at the title and says it was once her favorite book. That everyone should follow my example by having interests outside of schoolwork. It is embarrassing without being mortifying. After assembly the next day, Adena asks if I can recommend anything else to read, as *Jane Eyre* seems really silly to her. I tell her to take a look at *Pride and Prejudice*. She is always trying to start conversations with me, and I hope this book recommendation will put an end to that.

"Why does your brother sit on the fire escape?" she asks me.

"I don't know," I say. "I guess he and James like it up there."

"They seem really nice," Adena says. "You're lucky."

"How do you mean?" I ask, wondering why this cheerful and outgoing girl considers me lucky.

"I have an older brother and he's horrible," she says. "If he climbed up the fire escape, it would be to drop water balloons."

"Link and James would never do that," I tell her. "They don't believe in pranks."

"They're like a couple, aren't they?" Adena asks.

I ask where her brother goes to school and if she has any other siblings, and we stay off the topic of how very much like a couple Link and James are. A couple. Is that what they are? Is this what explains why I have spent so much time with them without ever knowing them?

They are a couple. Of course they are. And yet . . . I know enough about them to feel that this is not how they would choose to describe themselves. I could be wrong. Very wrong. I should ask them. An idea that is immediately terrifying. There is an excellent reason I have never thought of Link and James as a couple before; they have never permitted me to think of or to see them as anything other than friends.

I resolve never to ask them. Ever. I resolve to put it out of my mind. There is no reason for me to know. I don't need to ask in order to know that it's none of my business.

CHAPTER FIVE

O N SATURDAY I GET UP AS EARLY AS LINK DOES. HE wants to run his seven miles before going to what he and James call Maths for Freaks. I want to finally finish reading *Jane Eyre* before Mom and I go shopping. It's unbelievably good. Happy ending, unhappy characters whom I like, and parties with fires, fortunetellers, and last-minute guests. I wonder if James would ever love me the way Mr. Rochester loves Jane. I think of what Adena asked and realize how ridiculous it is to have a crush on James if he and Link are a couple.

Why would they have encouraged my crush on James if they could have stopped it by telling me they have a crush on each other? So they aren't a couple. No. Of course not. And yet . . . isn't what I dream of having with James exactly what he has with Link? A type of closeness that cannot—will not—reveal itself under scrutiny? They are a couple.

But wouldn't I know? This is *so* ridiculous. It's one thing for me to respect Link's desire to leave important information unsaid. It's quite another for me to be unable to tell myself critical facts about the people I love. I will tolerate bad grades but not this kind of ignorance. Surely I can follow Link's rules but also find things out. I will ask Mom. Someone who utilizes her talents and takes full advantage of all her opportunities will know the answers to questions I have never thought to ask.

Bloomingdale's blurs into Bergdorf's, and the Limited shifts to Barney's. Mom and I have radically different ideas about what looks good on me. We spend almost four hours buying five dresses, three of which I will never wear, four skirts, three pairs of pants, two pairs of jeans, four sweaters, and seven tops. Mom says I am impossible to shop for because I am too tall for things that should fit. That and the fact that she still thinks I am nine. She vetoed every short skirt I wanted, and the only tops we could agree on without a fight have little collars and button up to my chin. Ugh.

As I try things on and take them off, I work up the nerve to ask her. It takes me until we are leaving Barney's, and even then I don't exactly ask. Instead, I tell her about the fire escape (but not the smoking), what Adena said, and how I think I know but don't.

"Do you think Link's gay?" Mom says. "Is that what you want to know?"

She has stopped dead in the middle of the sidewalk. She almost never breaks her stride. When we were little we could never get her to stop.

"I don't know," I say. "I just wondered."

"I see," she says. "Have you asked him?"

"No," I say, annoyed that she is trying to dodge my question. "Have you?"

"No," she says. "I haven't. Do you want to talk about this?"

I nod. Sure, of course.

We settle into a restaurant a few blocks uptown on Madison Avenue. Mom orders a pot of tea and butter cookies. She asks if I want the chocolate layer cake or the triple chocolate mousse. I'm surprised, since she usually tries to keep me from eating dessert. I pick the cake.

"I don't know if your brother is gay," Mom says, pouring milk into the bottom of her cup. "It's clear to me he and James love each other. Link seems happy more often than not."

For this we had to get tea and cake?

"They are both very young," Mom says. "I'm not sure they know."

"Would you care if they were?" I ask.

"No. I care that Link's happy. Your father, on the other hand, cares very much. It's one of many reasons that I have never broached the subject with Link."

She doesn't want to have another argument with Dad about Link. If Dad cares, that must mean he thinks Link is gay. What does being gay mean anyway, other than being a boy who is like a couple with another boy?

"Has Dad asked Link?"

"No, of course not," Mom says. "Your father has many wonderful qualities. Direct discourse is not one of them."

I wish I remembered more about that fight my parents had. The one Link said almost caused a divorce. I am not anxious to force either of them into a repeat of that. I resolve to drop the whole matter. It doesn't matter if James and Link are a couple. I will remain *totally madly in love* with James no matter what.

"You could ask," Mom says, interrupting my decision making. "And you should. What if Link thinks nobody cares enough to ask him?"

"What if Link thinks it's nobody's business?" I ask.

"If you want to know your brother better, you have to be willing to let him know that."

As if by not asking Link, I don't want to know him. That's not fair.

"Yes," I say, wanting to yell at her that if she has many reasons for not asking Link, I might do well to follow her example.

"I know Link can be a difficult person to talk to," Mom says. "He is very like his father, but they are both worth every effort."

"Hmmmm," I say, no longer wanting to yell, just frustrated that I am not going to get an answer from anyone other than my prickly, secretive brother.

"If you want to know, you should ask," Mom says. "Both Link and James."

I nod. Okay, okay.

"You should always feel free to talk to me, Ellen. About anything. Your father and I love you both. No matter what."

"I know," I say in a pleasant and evasive manner.

They do love us. It's nice. I would rather have them for parents than Mr. and Mrs. Wentworth, but all this has been so very beside the point of the information I am seeking.

When we get home, Dad and Link demand a fashion show. Link has an ice pack over his eyes. Maths for Freaks gives him a headache. Dad is reading what he has been reading for years: a three-volume novel in German. We aren't supposed to talk about how it's taking Dad forever to read it. Or that he uses a dictionary when he's having trouble with his German. We're supposed to understand that this is how he relaxes when he's not cooking.

I model all twenty-five items of clothing, knowing that none of them will make me different. Dad says I look drop-dead gorgeous in everything. Mom looks relieved and exhausted. She says she needs a cup of tea as if we have not just spent half an hour drinking tea.

"And a brandy," she says.

Dad gets her the brandy and sends us into the kitchen to make tea. Link tells me there's nothing wrong with my new clothes, but that they would all look better on an eleven-year-old.

"Nine-year-old," I say.

"You're her baby," Link says.

I shrug. It could be worse. She could *not* care that I was growing up and getting closer and closer to leaving. The way Link will. In less than a year.

"I'll miss you," I say. "When you go to MIT, it will be awful."

"It won't be so bad," he says. But because it will be and he knows it, he tells me to come with him to James's house. Mr. and Mrs. Wentworth are out, and we can use the TV in their bedroom, which is a foot wider than the one in our living room. Even though it's already October, the weather is like springtime, and so we walk across town from the corner of Seventieth Street and Central Park West to Park Avenue between Eighty-ninth and Ninetieth Streets. The Wentworths live only three blocks from school.

James congratulates me on having survived an entire day shopping, and he gives Link two Advils along with one of Mr. Wentworth's imported beers. We have to order out because there is never anything to eat in the Wentworths' kitchen unless you like water crackers and cocktail onions. Link and James want Indian food and I want Japanese, so we compromise and order from a coffee shop:

hamburgers for them, grilled cheese with bacon for me, and lots of mashed potatoes for sharing. James opens two more bottles of beer and asks if I want one.

"Do you have ginger ale?" I ask, sounding like a nine-year-old.

He finds a jar of maraschino cherries and puts four of them into a glass of tonic water. As far as I'm concerned, there is no good time to ask this question, but how else will I ever know? I wait until they have decided what video to watch. It's a sequel to a German movie about angels. If I am remembering correctly, it was a very long movie in which the angels walked through a library in Berlin. I had better ask before the sequel starts, or it will be two in the morning and then too late.

I spear a cherry with an unused fork (James always puts out his mother's good silver) and ask if they are a couple.

"A couple of what?" Link asks me. "Geniuses? Or retards?"

"That's not what she means," James says.

"I guess I know what she means," Link says. "She's my sister."

"So answer her then," James says.

Link doesn't say anything. James studies Link, who is suddenly transfixed with what is on his plate. This was a mistake, I think. Big mistake.

"Why are you asking?" James asks me.

Mom told me to doesn't seem like the best answer in light of how quiet Link is.

"Adena said you were like a couple, and I didn't know if it was okay to agree with her or not," I say.

Long silence. I can hear the blood rushing and beating around my ears.

"Yes, it's okay," James says finally.

"It's not okay," Link says.

There is more silence, and I wonder if they are going to be able to settle this without speaking.

"Maybe you should tell her why it's not okay," James says.

"I don't have to tell her anything," Link says.

"No, of course not," I say. "I'm sorry, I just, I was wonder—"

"Then maybe you should tell me," James says, interrupting.

"You know why," Link says.

"I would like to hear it."

"Right this minute?"

"I have nothing to hide from Ellen," James says. "About anything. Can you say the same?"

Furious, Link turns to me. "I am not gay," he says. "James is gay."

"She didn't say anything about being gay," James says. "My God, she's like your clone. She didn't even utter the word."

"She implied it," Link says. "You told me to answer her and I did. I answered her implied question."

"Then answer this: What makes me gay and not you?" James asks.

"You've slept with people," Link says.

This is much more than I want to know. I stand up, prepared to go.

"Sit down," James says. "You can't only have the fun."

I sit down.

"Let her go," Link says. "I don't want to talk about this in front of Ellen."

"You don't want to talk about this in front of me either," James says.

"Correct," Link says. He is so mad his lips are white. "There's nothing to discuss. I'm going home."

"Go," James says. "If there's nothing to discuss, there's nothing to keep you here."

Link stands up and looks at me. It's very obvious he wants me to come with him. But it's even more obvious that if I do leave, I will never find out what it is he is going to such great lengths to avoid. I know if I stay, Link will never forgive me. And curiosity beats out loyalty by more than I would have guessed.

"I'm staying," I say.

"That's great," Link says, grabbing his stuff. "Just great."

He slams out of the apartment so hard that a picture frame in the front hall shatters to the floor. And here is my birthday wish spread before me. I should have been smart and stuck to not having one.

CHAPTER SIX

JAMES WON'T LET ME HELP HIM CLEAN UP THE BROKEN glass. He says I might cut my fingers and that if I'm really anxious to help, I should clear the table. Throw the food out. He sure is not hungry. By the time James has put away the now unframed poster (from a Vermeer exhibit in Amsterdam), I have cleaned everything up.

"This wasn't your fault," James says, sitting down at the kitchen table and motioning for me to do the same.

"It wasn't not my fault," I say, sitting down and thinking how it was Mom's fault. *If you want to know, you should ask.*

"Link and I have been needing to have this conversation for some time," he says.

"You didn't have a conversation," I say, in case he thinks people stomping out is any kind of talking.

"We had enough," James says. "Our positions are clear now."

Positions on what? Being a couple? If one of them says no, does that mean they aren't a couple, or is it proof that they are? And what's the big deal anyway? Part of me has been freaking out since Adena said James and Link were a couple, and I have no clear idea of why.

"Is that all it means?" I ask, stumbling through my confused, crowded, and ever cautious brain for the right question.

"Is what all?"

"Being gay," I say, thinking of how Mom said that Link and James love each other and that Link seems happy more often than not. She didn't say anything about sleeping together. And in *The Age of Innocence* Newland loved the Countess and only got to hold her hand twice. It took more than two hundred pages for Jane and Mr. Rochester to even say they loved each other. Forget sleeping together.

"What about being gay?" James asks. "Could you be more specific?"

"Is it the sex that makes you gay? Was Link right?"

I am about to ask why Link hasn't slept with anyone. Why Link hasn't, for instance, slept with James. If sex were the one thing separating me from James, I would do it. Wouldn't Link? I suddenly realize that I am sitting in an apartment with the object of my imaginary love life. Talking to him about sex. I am immediately mortified into silence.

"I need a cigarette," James says. "And a drink."

"We don't have to talk about this," I say. "It's none of my business."

"It kind of is your business," he says. "Aside from Link, you're probably my closest friend."

James is the closest I have ever had to any friend. I don't know how to tell him that and so I nod.

"And if it's not asking too much," James says, "I would like to cure at least one McConnell of the belief that saying nothing means there's nothing to say."

He goes out of the kitchen, and when he comes back he has his cigarettes and a bottle of Sambuca. He pours the Sambuca into two shot glasses he gets from the pantry. He raises his glass to mine and they clink. It tastes like a mixture of licorice, Seven-Up, and fire.

"I'm not an expert," he says, "but I don't think sex is the thing that makes someone gay."

"What does?"

"It's more whom you love," James says. "The how and why of it. And if what you get back is worth what you give up."

What is he talking about?

"Is Link?" I ask, putting aside the question of what makes someone gay.

"Is Link what?" James asks.

"Gay," I say, being specific. "Is he gay?"

"He doesn't know," James says. "Which makes him afraid he is. Which makes him swear he isn't."

"Are you?" I ask, realizing yet again that I am not

45

going to get an answer about my brother. I might as well find out about James.

"I don't know either," James says, pouring us both another glass. "It doesn't scare me, though."

"Was it true what he said?" I ask, unable to be specific.

"Yes, I've slept with people," he says, knowing what I've asked. "Men."

"Why never with a girl?" I ask, my brain suddenly so flooded with Sambuca there is no room for caution.

"Two reasons. A girl has never asked me and I never thought sleeping with a girl would annoy your brother."

I want to ask why James's sleeping with men would annoy Link if, as Link says, he himself is not gay. But it's so clear while also being confusing. Link was mad about James and the waiter, but he couldn't say that flat-out without retreating from his position that he's not gay. My brother has really boxed himself into a corner here.

Did it never occur to him to just sleep with James and thus avoid any conversation about what they were doing? It would be the Link-like thing to do. Although it sounds like it wasn't the sex that divided them. More the fact that Link is afraid and James isn't.

"It's not that I don't like girls," James says. "I do."

"Which girls?" I ask, reviewing the ones who told me to tell him hi. None of them deserve to sleep with James.

"Just generic girls. That's why I have no idea if I'm gay."

"Does Link like girls?"

"You know, we make a big point of not talking about

46

them," James says. "Girls don't interest me compared with Link. But compared with Link, men don't interest me either. All in all, though, girls are . . . girls have interesting qualities."

I am a girl. And I have my interesting qualities. I can't think of any, of course, but I must have some. When I sober up I will make a list of all my interesting qualities.

"But you love Link," I say to remind myself that when compared with Link, my qualities are irrelevant.

"It's hard to love Link," James says. "It's not something he encourages."

"He loves you," I say, no longer as sure about that as I was an hour ago.

"He has no clue what he feels," James says. "About me or math or college. Anything."

"I should go home," I say, not wanting to believe that my brother, the genius, is clueless.

"Tell him we played cards," James says, putting out his third cigarette. "And that I said I was sorry."

"I don't even know the rules to gin rummy," I say. "He'll know I'm lying."

"Tell him we watched a video, then. Just tell him I'm sorry."

"It's not your fault," I say.

"It's not Link's either," James says. "He'll want to hear that."

James rings downstairs on the intercom and tells the doorman to hail a cab. Then he takes a twenty-dollar bill out of his wallet and puts it in my hand.

"I love how you guys never have any money," he says.

Link and I get an allowance, but Dad taxes it so that we'll have money saved for things like Christmas and birthdays. It's to make us financially responsible, but as far as I can tell it's only made us financially dependent on Mr. and Mrs. Wentworth. They give James a huge allowance, which is not taxed.

When I get home, Link is in the living room watching *That Hamilton Woman*. Mom and Dad are out. They spend Saturday nights together doing something without us. It's what they call their night off. I ask Link if he wants something from the kitchen.

"No," he says. "You want to watch? Churchill's speech is about to start."

I say sure and sit down for the umpteenth time to watch Laurence Olivier as he delivers his first address in Parliament. When the movie ends and Link has hit "rewind," I ask again if he wants something from the kitchen.

"Do I look crippled to you?" he asks.

"No," I say. "I was just . . . asking."

"Don't," he says, and I know by his voice that he is saying more, but I did promise James. And he did say it twice. Almost three times.

"James said to tell you he was sorry."

"I'll bet he is," Link says, and he sounds as if he is talking to Mom instead of to me.

I want to ask him what my interesting qualities are. To

tell him that I'm sorry too. How I have never fully understood the two of them and that I see now it's because they don't understand themselves. I want to explain all this and have everything explained, and because I can't get the words out, I touch Link's arm. He jerks away from me as if I have burned him.

"Listen, Ellen, I only want to say this once. And I don't want to talk about it, and I don't want to find out that you've talked to Mom and Dad about it."

Right. As if my talking to Mom or Dad would ever lead to their talking directly to Link. It won't even lead to their talking directly to me. Can he be so totally unaware of this? Link hits "eject" on the VCR and snatches at his video before the machine has fully spit it out.

"Tell your little friend that James and I are not a couple."

"She thought it was a nice thing," I say.

"Of course she did," Link spits out at me. "Adena Cohen's father is a faggot. She has to think that."

Faggot is one of the many words that I know are used instead of the pleasant-sounding *gay*, whose definition has totally eluded me tonight. There are a bunch of these words: *queer, queen, fairy*. How come I know this awful list and not very much else about what *gay* means? How does Link know anything about Adena Cohen? How can anyone's father be gay, and why am I so incredibly stupid?

"*Faggot* isn't a very nice word," I say at last, totally

disgusted with my inability to think of something more pertinent.

"I am not gay," Link says, his voice very-end-of-discussion.

"Who would care if you were?" I ask, my voice shaking from nerves and fatigue and alcohol.

"I would," he says, sliding the video into its case.

When, on Sunday, James calls and Link refuses to come to the phone and James says a string of swear words before hanging up, I know nothing is the same anymore. James was right when he said I couldn't just have the fun. I hadn't realized that they couldn't either.

CHAPTER SEVEN

I SPEND A COUPLE OF WEEKS IGNORING MY HOMEWORK in an attempt to increase what I know about gay people. After a brief session with my computer during which I see pictures I would prefer not to know about, I stick to books. There's nothing in the school library by or about gay people except plays by Oscar Wilde and Tennessee Williams. Oscar Wilde died in prison and Tennessee Williams drank himself to death, I think.

I take what's saved from my taxed allowance and head downtown. There is a gay bookstore on West Nineteenth Street called A Different Light.

"Is it your father?" the woman working there asks me after establishing that I am not gay. Or worried about being gay.

"No," I say, trying to explain how the list of nasty

words (without actually using any of the words, of course) is all I know and how that seems needlessly ignorant of me. She shows me lots of things and gives me a fifteen percent discount.

"It's the price break we give to all straight people who want to educate themselves," the woman says as she rings up my selections.

I learn lots of things. Michelangelo was gay. Oscar Wilde went to prison for being gay (he died in Paris) but was married and had children. It used to be against the law for men to have sex with each other. People got arrested, lost their jobs, were abandoned by their friends, were put in mental homes, or killed themselves. A math genius who helped Britain beat the Nazis was rewarded by losing his security clearance when the government found out he was gay.

Now it's not a big deal. There's AIDS to worry about or getting attacked by a redneck, but that's about it. Only people who don't know better still think it's shameful or wrong to be gay, but not people we know. Not smart people. Which makes me think there's something seriously wrong with Link. Why the nuclear meltdown at my asking if he and James were a couple? James said Link was afraid. Afraid of what? Link's too smart to think like the people I've read about. The religious zealots and other people who don't know better.

I keep reading because I'll never be able to ask. The Link I would follow anywhere walked out of the Wentworths' apartment that night and has yet to return. The Link who remains is not speaking to me. And he suddenly has a girlfriend. Laurel's sister Polly. I hear her voice on the phone almost every night: quiet, polite, nervous, and unbelievably happy.

"Hi, it's Polly Keller calling. May I please speak to Link?"

And she does. For hours. Judging by my brother's side of the conversation, he can't get a word in edgewise. Or he simply can't be bothered to comment on what she has to say. At school, I see them in the courtyard, where they sit with a bunch of Polly's friends. It's a group made up of a few of the popular boys from eleventh grade and most of the girls who wanted me to tell James hi.

At lunch, Link and Polly sit at a big table in the middle of the cafeteria with the exact same people. Link doesn't look unhappy, but neither does he look like his animated self the way he did in James's company.

James, meanwhile, does not approve of my research project. "It's not worrying he's gay that explains Link's behavior," he says.

"What is it then?" I ask.

"It's me," James says. "He didn't think he could trust me."

"Why?" I ask. James was Link's best friend. "How could he not trust you?"

"Who knows how his mind works," James says, his shrug disdainful. "These ridiculous books about gay people won't tell you that. You're wasting your time."

It's my time to waste, after all, and I want to know about these things I have managed to spend fourteen years never thinking about. I keep reading but hide my books from James. He remains on the fire escape during the courtyard break, but we eat together. As the days turn into many weeks, he says that my sitting with him is making it impossible for Link to forgive me. He himself is done with the cafeteria.

"You can't leave me sitting by myself," I say, in full panic.

"Go sit with those girls," he says. "They like you. Let them like you."

"One of them is Polly Keller's sister," I say. "If I sit with her, I'll have to listen to her talking about how adorable Link is."

I hear enough of this in the courtyard when Adena and Laurel repeat Polly repeating Link. It's awful. Not to mention I would eat my own hand to avoid any prolonged contact with Adena. If Link is right, she knows more than I do about what *gay* means. I am not confident that I could talk to Adena without inadvertently betraying the uncertainties that my brother harbors in secret and with fear.

"Then we have to eat out," James says. "Because I can't watch him with that girl."

I see in his face how tired and angry he is from *not* watching Link with Polly.

"Ninth graders have to get parental permission to leave the building," I say.

54

"We're going to work around that," James says. "In the top drawer of your dad's messy desk is a stack of his stationery. Bring me some."

"Why?" I ask, when what I mean is, how do you know this? Why do you know this? What are you doing?

"So I can write a note from your father requesting that you be able to go out for lunch," James says. "I've done his signature for your brother quite a few times."

I sit in the study for a while before taking Dad's stationery. I know that he would expect better from me. I am, in his eyes, a good girl. Just as, in Mom's eyes, I am nine. A good nine. Save for my lack of social skills, I have conformed to what they both want in a daughter. My hand hovers over the desk drawer. It's not getting caught that makes me hesitate. It's the fear of becoming someone other than the person Mom and Dad think they know. Finally, it comes down to wanting to eat lunch with James more than wanting to keep my parents happy. I take several sheets to school and watch the name *Colin A. McConnell* flow from James's pen. As a way of compensating, I put my books by and about gay people aside. I reacquaint myself with my homework, my father's academic expectations, and my own desire not to garner too much attention.

By midterms, I have hit the B I was aiming for in all of my classes. This is where not being the Second Coming of Lincoln McConnell becomes the curse I've been dreading. Half my teachers think I am working below my potential. I am the sister of a whiz kid. Surely I can do better than this. They expect an A. The other half think I am struggling too hard to keep up. I am the sister of a whiz kid. Clearly he got all the brains, and I am killing myself to turn in a decent performance. They expect a C.

Dad, who is in London or San Francisco or wherever his uniquely important meeting is, isn't so busy that he forgets to call the school for our grades. He then calls home to let us know what he thinks of our performance. To Link, he says, "The school says most seniors act like they're done already. I'm glad you're still earning your wings." After Link switches the speakerphone off and hands me the receiver, he sticks his arms out, weaving from side to side as if he were an airplane.

"Plenty of room for improvement, Ellen," Dad says. "But they think you're adjusting really well."

"I'm trying," I say, thinking, listen, I worked hard for those Bs you want improved.

"Good girl," he says. "At least those ridiculous reports on your social abilities have stopped."

"At least," I say, wishing he hadn't put it quite like that.

"In the long run, it's your effort that makes you who you are," Dad says.

"He thinks I could improve," I say to Link after I hang up.

"Couldn't we all," he says, pretending to fly out of the study with his arms.

Ms. Detert, at least, is totally happy with me. I am getting a B in French because it is easy and because I trust her never to call on me for an answer. James says that if I keep it up, he will take me to Paris in June. Mr. and Mrs. Wentworth have promised to send him there as a graduation present.

"That's nice of them," I say.

"They are nothing if not nice people," James says.

"By June, you and Link will be back to normal," I say. "His French is way better than mine."

"His company leaves something to be desired," James says.

"Do you think I should give him some of the books I've read?"

"I thought you had stopped, Ellen. Reading is not going to explain Link to you."

"Maybe he doesn't know that it's not a big deal to be gay."

"It's a big enough deal," James says. "My parents make me see a shrink because they're worried I'm gay."

People used to think that being gay was a mental illness, but doctors (*especially* psychiatrists) no longer believe that. Even if Mr. and Mrs. Wentworth aren't fit to be parents, I've never heard Mom call them stupid. I ask James if his parents know that reasonable people don't think being gay is a mental illness.

"They do know," he says. "They send me so I can make my own choices without being influenced by their deep desire that I be straight."

"Why is that their desire?"

"Because no one wants their kid to be gay."

"Mom doesn't care," I say.

"Your mother may not, but check with your father," James says.

I think of my beside-the-point conversation with Mom. *Your father, on the other hand, cares very much.* I was so busy thinking about how Mom and Dad might have another fight that I didn't ask her why Dad cares very much.

"Why would Dad care?" I ask, reluctant to reveal that he does. "It's not against the law anymore."

"No one gets arrested anymore," he says. "But it's not exactly legal."

"All those laws were overturned," I say. "So it is legal."

"Ellen, there are a ton of laws that no one wants to admit exist," James says. "Laws that monitor behavior."

I think of Newland in *The Age of Innocence* and how he was kept from his every desire by what society expected. How it was all unspoken but clear.

"You mean social laws?" I ask.

"Yes," James says. "They're unwritten laws, so they never get overturned, but everyone is expected to obey them."

"What happens if you refuse to?" I ask, wondering if that's why my old school used to send notes home. Perhaps my "failure to connect" disobeyed an unwritten social law.

"You get punished," he says. "Not arrested, but enough to make you worry."

I have, of course, missed learning about these particular laws in my reading. No one writes them down because that would involve admitting they exist. Everyone has to learn what they are and how to cope with them in their own way. The unwritten social laws about gay people might be ones that Dad, despite being smart and someone I know, obeys. And he probably wants us to obey them as well. The way he wants us to obey his laws about our minds and their heartbeats.

"You think Dad told Link that it was wrong?"

"I don't know," James says. "Maybe. Yes. Of course he did."

Of course he did. And being Dad, he did it without ever having to say anything.

How is it that my father, whom I think I know so well, has picked the wrong—the ignorant—laws to follow? How would Link—how would I—ever follow laws different from Dad's if his are the ones we learn first?

"So Link has a good reason for being so . . . awful."

"Ellen, he is your brother, and you are not allowed to think he's awful."

James signals for the check. We are at Sarabeth's, which is where we usually eat lunch, since it is less than a block from school.

"He's not talking to me," I say. "I can think whatever I want."

"He'd talk to you if he could figure out how never to mention my name," James says. "We need to think of what you can do with him that involves neither me nor the unfortunate Polly Keller."

"Math?"

"You want to keep far away from your brother and math," James says. "How about running?"

"He'll never go for it," I say. "He'll know I don't want to run. That it's just to be with him."

"It's not your wanting to be with him that he minds," James says. "It's your demanding to know him."

Perhaps people have their own personal unwritten laws in addition to the social ones. And one of Link's laws could be that no one is allowed to know him well. In which case both James and I have broken it. Tried to, at least. The punishment for our efforts to know Link seems clear enough: banishment. If I have to choose, I would rather be with my brother than know him.

CHAPTER EIGHT

IT SO HAPPENS THAT I AM REALLY GOOD AT RUNNING. For all that I am clumsy in my normal life (and I am— my knees love to bang into corners and my elbows to knock against walls), I have it together while running. We don't talk much. Just move and breathe, with Link occasionally telling me "turn left" or "land on your heels." Somewhere in Central Park, while watching my feet keep pace with his, I realize that Link and I have never been big talkers.

Before Link met James, my brother and I spent time together giving each other quiet company. I would watch him build model planes, cars, or ships. He might read me a story—skipping over the sections he deemed dull—or help me build a palace from an ancient set of building blocks. We didn't sit around chatting. It was only after

James entered the picture that I heard Link talk a lot. Now I know that much too much was going unsaid, but without James around I would never have heard Link's opinions on movies, books, other people, or music.

The running is a lot like an old memory, even though I have never done it before. When we finish, Link says I can come with him again whenever I want. I am, it would seem, forgiven. Up to a point. There are definitely things he does not wish to discuss with me, but I do get a formal introduction to Polly.

"I hear you hate reading movies as much as I do," Polly says.

"I usually *watch* movies," I say, "although I have been reading a lot."

"She means foreign films," Link says.

"I don't hate foreign films," I say. "In fact, I love subtitles. They make it possible for the linguistically challenged to enter another culture."

I heard James say that once, and I always remembered it because of how the phrase "linguistically challenged" made Link laugh. He doesn't find it funny today.

"She's making that up," Link says to Polly, his voice a glare I know well.

"Well, it's certainly something I'll keep in mind," Polly says to me.

When I tell James about my sudden love for foreign films, I am rewarded by a hidden smile.

"Shall we test this newfound love of yours?" James asks.

There is an Iranian film festival at Film Forum. Two of the best films are on Saturday. Do I want to go?

"Are the films in Iranian?" I ask, dreading hours of subtitles.

"Persian. Modern Persian. Better known as Farsi."

I am all caught up at school. I am reading *Wuthering Heights*, which Mom said I would love and Dad said was a ridiculous book. I'm not in a big hurry to finish it and deliver an opinion that disappoints one of them. Dad leaves for Rome on Sunday (yet another important meeting), and a lot of Mom's deadlines are coming closer. The McConnell family dinner hour is on hiatus again, leaving behind the bad mood of broken resolution. Getting out of the house—even for Farsi—sounds good.

Link and I run on Saturday morning, and I meet James after my brother has gone to Maths for Freaks. The two movies we see are as long and boring as I dreaded. We take a cab back uptown to James's favorite restaurant. He wants to buy me dinner.

"I know you were in agony," he says.

"It wasn't so bad," I say.

"You are a terrible liar," he says. "Worse than your brother."

James orders a beer with dinner. He has a fake ID but never gets carded. I pick around my dinner, thinking of the conversation he could be having with Link if Link

63

were still himself. In the cab, James said he thought the films were evocative but lacked a visual coherence. I know Link would have agreed or disagreed. I, however, have no idea what James meant.

"What does *visual coherence* mean?" I ask him.

"It's a pretentious way of saying I didn't think the images held together."

"Oh," I say, feeling defeated. "Held together for what?"

"For the story. A movie should have a visual vocabulary."

This is awful. What is a visual vocabulary? Subtitles? "I'm sorry," I say. "I don't know what you're talking about. I can't think as well as Link."

"You think differently from the way he does. It's not a better or worse type of thing."

"It would be more fun if I thought the way he did," I say.

"I'm not sitting here wishing you were your brother," James says. "You have your own worthwhile traits, Ellen."

"Does that mean I have interesting qualities?" I ask, all in a rush. It's as if the question has been living in my throat since I heard him say he liked girls.

"Yes," he says gently. "Of course you do."

"What are they?"

"Are you flirting with me?" he asks.

"No," I say.

"You're not?"

"No," I repeat.

"You've outgrown me," James says.

"No," I say. "It's the kind of thing I would have asked Link to list for me. I've been wondering for weeks what mine are."

"They are too numerous to be captured on a list," James says. "Maybe I'll do a drawing of them."

"And I could see it?" I ask, knowing that only Link can see James's drawings.

"I'll give it to you," James says, counting out twenties to leave with the bill. "What are you doing tomorrow?"

"Homework."

"You want to come out with me instead?" James asks.

"Sure," I say. "Where?"

"I thought we'd work on your visual vocabulary."

"I won't go to a museum," I say. "Not even with you."

In a museum or gallery, I always feel as though the paintings are looking back at me. It's creepy.

"No," he says. "You can't learn to see there."

"I can see," I say, shrugging on my coat.

"You want to go to a hospital or an airport?"

"Hospital," I say, thinking how I've been to airports but never a hospital. "I can already see in both."

Seeing is not exactly what James has in mind. *Comprehension* is a better word for what he wants from me. We go to the cafeteria at NYU Medical Center on Thirty-fourth Street and so far east that it is almost on top of the FDR Drive. You can see the East River from the windows, but James says we are not here to look at the view.

"Why are we here?"

"To look at the people," he says.

There are groups of doctors sitting over plates of cold food and cups of coffee. You can tell they are doctors by the stuff falling out of their pockets: beepers, stethoscopes, and Filofaxes. At other tables, groups of lab technicians make a big point of not sitting with orderlies, who are the only people here who look happy. There are people sitting alone who don't look like patients but who obviously don't work here.

"Relatives," James says. "Friends. Outpatients. That kind of thing."

"Do you come here a lot?" I ask. "It's depressing."

"It's interesting, if you know how to look."

"You draw these people, don't you?"

"Yes," he says, looking alarmed but also delighted.

"So this is your version of a museum."

"A black velvet dress for parties," he says. "A blow dryer. Books from medical school in a pile by the desk because there's no more room on the shelves."

"What are you talking about?"

"I'm making a list," he says, "of all the things I think someone in here owns. You have to guess whom I've picked to observe."

"Everyone in the world has a blow dryer," I say, looking around the cafeteria for someone who owns lots of books and a black velvet dress.

"Not bald men," James says. "Bubble bath. Running shoes. A day planner that is usually missing."

I eliminate all the men in the room and all of the women who are either too fat, too busy, or too old to soak in a perfumed tub before dressing up. A woman is sitting a few tables over from us. She is wearing light blue scrubs, and her hair is falling out of its barrette. Just the way mine does.

"Her," I say, pointing.

"Don't point," he says. "Yes. You go."

I pick one of the non–doctors/patients who is old and has a beard. I think about his closet and his library. His medicine chest. His bedside table.

"A water glass he took from a hotel in London," I say. "Nail scissors. A tweed jacket."

James gives the location of my guy. We do this back and forth for about an hour. This is the most interesting room I've ever been in. I can't imagine thinking of it as depressing.

"Why don't we do this at school?" I ask.

"It works best with strangers," James says. "Strangers are like blank paper. You can draw what you please."

"Do you usually draw people after you've listed what they own?"

"Yes," he says. "Because then I've thought them through."

"And that's how you see better?" I ask.

"It's not better," James says. "It's just a way."

"Next time we come here, I'll bring my homework and you can draw after we're done seeing everybody."

"This isn't even the best hospital," James says. "Wait until you've hung out at Mount Sinai."

"I want to go to all of them," I say.

We spend every afternoon that week going to hospital cafeterias to see which has the best people. On Friday, we go to St. Vincent's cafeteria, which is downtown and my favorite. It has a patients' section. James doesn't like to think them through, saying it's not very polite. I disagree, and while I make lists in my mind (cats, designer ties, cell phone batteries, and lots of prescription bottles), James draws. Healthy people, I assume. I am looking at an old lady fold her walker (pink shawl, walking shoes, pain-killers) when James taps on my elbow, saying, "I guess this is for you."

He gives me the cardboard tube that has been sticking out of his bag all day. I pull a pencil drawing from the tube and smooth it on the table between us. It is of a girl dressed as a storybook princess. She's paused in a huge arched doorway, holding her skirt (as if it were in her way) while surveying the party going on in the ballroom before her. And it's some party: full of dancers, waiters, and people standing in groups. The princess is a dead ringer for me, and not because she's tall and skinny. My nose and mouth aren't exactly that shape, but her expression is one I see in the mirror every day.

"How did you do that?" I ask. "She looks just like me."

"Only a little like you," he says. "I had to cheat to get your qualities in it."

Because of the way she's holding it, there are folds in her skirt, and instead of a line, James has woven a word into each fold. *Curious, careful, kind,* and *intense.*

"You think I'm intense?"

"It's your most interesting quality," he says.

"I love this," I tell him. "My very own party."

"This is the only drawing I've ever given away."

I tell him it's going up on my wall.

"It will be the first thing I see in the morning," I say, meaning: *I love you. Thank you. You're wonderful.*

Perhaps he hears what I mean, for his smile looks like it's never hidden anywhere in its life.

CHAPTER NINE

I HAD A GROWTH SPURT IN THE SEVENTH GRADE: FOUR and a quarter inches in five months. I went from being average height to two inches shy of the six feet I currently am. My hips hurt, I slept a lot, and I only had one pair of pants which fit, but other than that there was no obvious change. I saw myself every day. There was no way to notice how tall I was until I went to the pediatrician and she said, "Ellen, you've gotten really big."

This is what it feels like to see my brother with Polly at the same time that I see James alone and off school grounds. During the weeks leading up to Thanksgiving, I know something is changing, but I feel the same. James says I look the same. Link, who looks thin and drawn to me, doesn't say much except that I should seriously consider joining the track team.

Christmas is a private family event, but Thanksgiving is a business opportunity. Dad always invites what he calls the orphans of his staff, anyone whose family is far away and/or hasn't been invited elsewhere. This year seven people are coming. Dad has been so busy traveling for work that he's having the turkey and the pies catered. It really pains him to do that, but Thanksgiving won't happen otherwise.

I unpack the food that has been delivered so that Dad can focus on what he *is* cooking. Link is working in the dining room because applying to college demands more space than even a neat desk can afford. The headmaster wants completed college applications before exams start. He needs time to match students to teachers for the required recommendations.

Mom is at a last-minute meeting with the manager of the Locust Club. There is a drapes emergency. I think she will probably work through the weekend. Dad is chopping up stale bread, walnuts, and celery for stuffing. He'll make it tonight and serve it with the turkey tomorrow.

"How's school?" he asks, opening a bag of dried cran-berries.

"It's okay," I say reluctantly. I'm so behind in my homework it's not funny. Instead of doing assignments, I'm reading a lot of art books in the hope that one day I can really look at paintings the way I now really look at people. It's the kind of reading I have to do in bits and

71

pieces. It's not all interesting, but neither is it all boring.

"Are you enjoying your new friends?"

My friends. I wasn't expecting this question from him. "How do you mean?"

"Don't look so panic-stricken, Ellen," Dad says. "I'm only trying to get a sense of your life. It seems like I was just teaching Link fractions, and now he has a girlfriend and does math I can't understand."

"Link taught himself fractions," I remind Dad. "It's why he skipped third grade."

"I was speaking metaphorically," Dad says. "You guys change so fast. With you, I have a shot at staying one step ahead."

He has no idea how Link has changed. And if he thinks he's a step ahead of me, he should think again.

"I like school," I say. "Everything's fine. When I finish *Wuthering Heights*, I'll read those short stories by Colette that you said were so good."

"Novellas," Dad says and then, obviously done asking about me, asks what I think of Polly.

Mom has asked me this too. In a manner that gave no indication that we had ever talked about the exact nature of James and Link's relationship. And yet, she asked about Polly in terms of James. Why doesn't Link bring her home? After all, James was here constantly. I used a pleasant and evasive manner to avoid answering Mom. Now my father wants to know what I think of Polly. How did we get off the topic of *Wuthering Heights*?

"Polly thinks Link is adorable," I say finally.

"You make that sound like a bad thing," Dad says.

"James knows Link is a genius," I say. "There's a difference."

"One can't have everything," he says, laughing.

I no longer feel bad about not being the good girl he thinks he knows. I only wish I had done more than take stationery. I wonder why I have always assumed that if I didn't know what my father was talking about, it meant I was the one who was clueless. I should tell him what I have really been reading. The books before my unmentioned art books.

I could talk about how I am at least six steps ahead of him when it comes to coping with the unwritten social laws about gay people. But I am reluctant to have a disagreement or, worse and more likely, an argument with my father. Even if he is clueless, I don't want to disappoint him. And anyway, the talk with Dad about gay people surely belongs more to my brother than to me. I stay in the kitchen until he starts grating ginger to put into the sweet potatoes tomorrow. Fresh ginger smells good, but it looks like a rotted tree root.

Thanksgiving (a.k.a. the business opportunity) goes inexplicably well. Mom acts as if she's interested in something other than fabric patterns. Link and I answer the bazillion questions Dad's friends ask as a way of proving to him how interested they are in us. Link sounds cheerful as he talks about Stanford, MIT, and the merits of other colleges. I am pleased that four of the seven grownups say they loved *Jane Eyre*, and every one of them said they would have to give Edith Wharton another look.

I serve the pies and Link takes orders for coffee, decaf, and three kinds of tea. When the phone rings, Link excuses himself to get it, and when he comes back, some ten minutes later, he is not in a good mood.

"For you," he says from the doorway.

Dad, Mom, and I all stand up. "Ellen," he says and disappears. I ask to be excused and Mom nods. Everyone is almost done or else she'd send me to bring Link back to the table.

I go into Dad's study, where the phone is still off the hook.

"Hey," I hear James say. "You guys in the middle of eating?"

"No," I say. "What happened with Link? You've ruined the first good mood he's had in months."

"Can't have been that good of a mood if I could ruin it," James says.

"It was good enough," I say. "What happened?"

"It wasn't such a great conversation that I want to have it twice," James says. "I thought you might want to spend some time tomorrow finally getting use out of your Rollerblades."

"Okay," I say. "Sure."

He tells me where in the park to meet him. Members

of the Coven are coming to visit his father tomorrow. The Coven is what James calls his three half sisters. They are from his father's first marriage. The youngest one is thirty-one but was my age when James was born. Mrs. Wentworth was already pregnant when she married Mr. Wentworth. The Coven, somewhat understandably, don't like James's mother. James doesn't like them at all. He'd rather be out when they visit. He asks if I can find a way to be free for dinner as well.

I fall three times blading to the band shell. Thank God Mom made me wear my helmet and knee pads. I don't mind falling so much, but falling while moving is a drag. James is already there doing lazy, loopy figure eights, and I watch him for a while. James is skinny like Link and me, but more graceful.

It's as if he were used to his body the way I was to mine before I left "average height" behind in the dust. The fact that he is astonishingly good-looking is something you can tell from a distance. When he catches sight of me, I see people stop and turn as he blades in my direction.

"Well, look at you," he says. "Ready to break a limb?"

"So it would seem," I say.

James shows me how to stop while turning. How to turn on a straight line. How to fall backward instead of forward. It involves shifting your weight as you go down, instead of struggling to balance.

"Accept the inevitable," he says.

I bang down onto my knees eleven times before my body understands what my brain has been told.

"You got it," James says. "Now let's call it a day."

After I work them off, James knots my Rollerblades to his and swings them over his shoulder. I strip off my pads and he puts them in his knapsack. He rummages deeper into his bag, pulling out a sweater, sketchbook, cigarettes, and his inhaler.

"I left my wallet at home," he says. "We're going to have to brave the Coven." He looks a little sick.

"Come to my house," I say. "There's a ton of food left over."

"No," James says. "It would be weird."

"It's more weird that you don't come," I say. "You and Link aren't going to be fighting forever."

"That's not why it would be weird."

"Then come. It can't be worse than the Coven."

"I don't think he should see us together."

"Why not?"

"For the same reason I prefer not seeing him with Polly."

"He's dating Polly," I say. "You aren't dating me."

"We're not dating," he says, "the way your brother and I weren't a couple."

I have a perfect memory of how James and Link used to prowl the hallways of school together. As if they were looking for something, when it was clear to anyone with eyes that they had found each other.

"It's totally different," I say. "You love Link."

76

"I don't not love you," James says, taking one of my hands in his and pretending that he only wants to warm it up.

"Well, it's different from the way you don't not love him," I say, wanting this to happen but terrified it will.

"It is different," he says.

He looks at me as if to check whether I'm going to jerk away from him. The way I imagine Link has jerked away from James many times.

"Have you outgrown me?" he asks, sliding a hand down my face.

Now I know what's different: I've outgrown the question. I am not attached to James solely through Link. And while he can no longer make me blush, I am old enough for James to break *my* heart. Breaking his when I outgrow him is no longer the only option.

"No," I say, not telling him it's the wrong question.

I don't move when James leans in to kiss me. I think of how little concrete knowledge the fifteen percent discount from the bookstore gave me. Of Newland Archer and his Countess. As I get used to kissing for real (so much better than the kind that happens only in my head), I think of James and his amazing face. I kiss him right back as if he were mine.

CHAPTER TEN

WHEN WE STOP, WE DON'T SAY ANYTHING. JUST kind of look at each other. Once I thought his face was mysterious, but now it is like a translucent screen. What I see there is what I've imagined seeing for almost two years. He looks happy because of me. It is different from how he was happy with Link, but it's as real.

"I should have waited," he says, looking away from me.

"Hmmmm," I say, as evasive as possible while my blood thumps around screaming: *Waited for what?*

"I knew this would happen, and I wanted everything to be okay with Link."

It dawns on me that this is the first time I have heard James say my brother's name since the night Link stomped out on us.

"You knew what would happen?" I ask.

He is silent for a very long time. I let the effects of my burning mouth and happy heart zip around my body.

"I used to call you *Our Insurance*," James says. "It drove him crazy, but we both knew that if you were around, certain things wouldn't—couldn't—happen."

"Our Insurance," I say. I was their insurance, and look at what I've done.

"Before we went to Maine, Link and I had a huge blowout. There was a guy from school. He'd been a senior and was kind of interested in me. Smart. Funny. Cute enough."

A senior. So he's in college this year. I hate him. I hate him for Link and for me.

"I asked Link what was the point of not letting someone love me. You know, someone who would let me love him. Could he give me one good reason not to go out with this guy? And your brother said, 'You have Ellen. Ellen loves you.'"

"But you knew that," I say. "You didn't need Link to tell you that."

"I hadn't realized until he said it that we were relying on you to be together," James says.

"How?" I ask, feeling a little weird. How is it that they relied on me when I looked to them for everything?

"We were never able to . . . um, express affection. It freaked him out. He thought it was the same thing as having sex. So I expressed it all to you. And you let me."

"What happened to the senior?" I ask, feeling less weird, but not as normal as I did before we kissed.

79

"Robert? He's at Emory."

"Did you like him?" I ask.

"Not enough," James says. "But I knew that eventually I would leave Link for someone who could show their love."

"You didn't leave Link for me," I say.

"Still, you are very wrapped up in my thinking that I could be with someone else."

"I can't be someone else," I say. "I can only hold Link's place."

I have never said it to myself like that, but all along I knew that's what I was doing. It's why my outgrowing James is beside the point. The point is more how I could want Link's place long past when he is ready to take it back.

"It's not Link's place for you to hold," James says. "It's mine to give away and I thought, I mean . . . isn't this what you want? Have I freaked you out now?"

There is real terror in his face now, and I kiss him because no one I love will ever be afraid on my account.

"This is what I want," I say, pulling away. "But there's all this stuff you want from Link. That he wants from you."

"The only thing Link wants from me is to be left alone," James says. "I did want things from him, but it made him unhappy. And crazy."

"What do you want from me?" I ask.

"The usual stuff," he says, a smile of shyness breaking free. "Love, attention. Bouts of intensity. You."

80

"So you're not gay?" I ask, meaning, compared to Link am I enough?

"Not any more than I ever was," James says.

I get that the thing that matters to him is what he can have with somebody. Be it a girl, a boy, a man, or a woman. Right now I am the someone he has. This doesn't make him straight, but it doesn't make him gay either. We leave it unsaid. Not because it is to be avoided, but because it is obvious.

James puts his sweater around my shoulders. The sun has started its hasty descent, and our bodies cast long, thin shadows.

"I'll walk you home," he says.

"What do I say to Link?"

"Anything you want," James says. "You can tell him I still love him but not in a way that will cause him alarm."

"Do I have to say anything?"

"No," he says. "I would let it alone."

We walk through the park and across the street toward my house.

"There's going to be weirdness with your brother," he says. "It's unavoidable."

James leaves me at the door. With the weirdness disguised as a kiss. I have his sweater. If he is to be believed, I have him. I resolve not to be alarmed.

During the weekend, Link turns the dining room table into a schizophrenic mess. On one side are papers, files, college catalogs, and books. On the other side are the scattered pieces from an old airplane model. His college essay is on how he hopes math will one day deliver the thrill he got from building these models. Mom says it's very good but that his use of commas is a tad too creative. Dad says the essay needs a more riveting style.

I have to ask to read it. It's not the style or the commas I notice, but the fact that it sounds like Link doesn't really like math. He liked building his models because he could observe what he was doing. The way he writes about math makes it sound like he is drowning in it. Not watching it at all. I have obviously missed the pertinent point. As always, when it comes to my brother.

I settle into the kitchen and confront my school books. Thanks to my various reading projects (*Wuthering Heights*, books about art, and books about sexual identity), I am hopelessly behind in all of my classes. I will manage a B minus in French and chemistry. English will totally depend on the essay question. History and math are beyond the pale. I give them up as lost, figuring that the worst that can happen is for Dad to realize that he is more than one step behind who I am. This is something I have, in fact, wished for. My exams will reveal a truer picture of the girl my parents think they know.

I spend the next few weeks in a fog of kissing and not kissing. I am amazed to discover that my entire life can be divided into these two categories. One afternoon, I go by myself to the NYU Medical Center's cafeteria. Instead of imagining what the people around me own, I try to picture them kissing. This quickly leads to my making a list of people who I know kiss.

Mom and Dad, which is a little yucky. Mr. and Mrs. Wentworth, which is fine, but they seem too busy to divide their lives up into kissing and not kissing. Link and Polly, which is hard to imagine. Link and James, which is not so hard to imagine and brings this particular list of mine to an abrupt end.

When I am with James, I feel way more drunk from the kissing than I felt from the Sambuca I had that night. I am reckless with affection. Physical affection. As if I can make up for what my brother would not offer. As if I could kiss away any unhappy moment James has ever had. James says he will not sleep with me. Not, repeat, not. It is too soon. We have moved really fast, he says, because of the unusual way we became friends. He will not take advantage of that. Not with me. This is what he says. It is not always what he does, and I stay in my fog of kissing and touching. Of not kissing and not touching.

Too soon, exams are upon us. James makes a half-hearted attempt to interest me in studying, but he is drafting and redrafting his own college essay. When he comes up for air, he is not so interested in my schoolwork.

His essay is about the summer he stayed with the Coven at a house in Nantucket. The house had been his father's before he lost it to the first Mrs. Wentworth in the divorce settlement. James was nine that summer, and his parents were on a six-week tour of Asia. Each sister let him know how she held his mother responsible for breaking up her parents' marriage. The essay is funny and sad and mean. It makes you feel horrible for James's mother, but also for the sisters. It makes you want to run a knife through Mr. Wentworth.

"You probably shouldn't show this to your father," I say.

"No kidding," James says. "But do you think it's good?"

"Yes," I say. "It has a riveting style."

"You're sweet, Ellen," he says, wrapping my hair around his fingers. "Intensely sweet."

James punctuates a lot of what he says by touching. We are sprawled across his bed, surrounded by drafts of his essay. I know that if James were somebody else, I would not fearlessly lie around on a bed with him. It amazes me how I have turned into a girl who worries about sex. Both having it and not having it. Less than a year ago, I was a girl bringing home notes that detailed my inability to socialize. And now James and I navigate around each other's bodies, trying to establish boundaries even as we erase them.

It's a strange pleasure, but not a frightening one. I have spent too much time in rooms where James sleeps to feel scared in one. Also, he tells me not to be scared.

He wraps his arms around me and rests his head against my shoulder or back. Whatever is handy.

"Don't be scared," he says. "Nothing bad will happen."

There is, as James said, "going to be weirdness with your brother." So I'm not scared that we are going to wind up going to bed just because we are *on* the bed. This particular weirdness will prevent some things while permitting others. I don't care exactly how it will work. No matter how far away I get from the girl my parents know, I won't be scared as long as I am with James.

CHAPTER ELEVEN

L INK TURNS HIS EXAMS IN BLANK. ALL OF THEM. THIS makes my Ds in English and algebra somewhat irrelevant. Also my inexplicable A in history. I am the only one home when the call comes. It's from Link's math teacher, Ms. Nolan.

"Where are your parents, Ellen?" she asks.

"Dad's in Europe," I say. "Mom's out."

"Out where?" she asks.

"Work," I say, not wanting to explain how living in Manhattan with two kids in private school is not cheap and that, therefore, Mom works all over the place. "Link will be back soon."

"I do not want to speak to Link," she says.

"May I take a message?" I ask, reaching for a pencil.

"Let me have your mother's cell phone number," Ms. Nolan says. Demands.

Mom calls about seven minutes later. She sounds horrible. As if she is choking from trying not to cry. She wants me to look up the folder on her laptop where she put Dad's itinerary.

"Do a search on the hard drive for Milan," she says.

"It's not here," I say, watching files spin by. "Have you tried his cell phone?" He doesn't like us to use it when he is in Europe, but this sounds serious enough.

"He's turned it off," Mom says, and then, "Call his office. They'll know. Where is your brother?"

"No idea," I say, which is not true. He is running, but I want to give Link an out.

It doesn't sound like Ms. Nolan had good news.

"He's turned his exams in blank," Mom says, finally crying. "Every single one. It's all so hostile."

Hostile to whom, I'd like to ask, but I don't. If Link wanted to say something about himself by doing this, he has picked the wrong venue. Mom and Dad will only see how this is about them.

"You could have told her where I was," Link says when he returns, sweating and frozen. "It's not like I was hiding it from them. I knew the school wouldn't keep it a secret."

"Why?" I ask. "Why did you do this?"

"I know everything I've studied this year," Link says. "My teachers know I know. Why should I write a bunch of junk just to prove what we all know?"

"Because an exam is proof," I say. "That's the whole point of an exam."

"It's a stupid point," Link says. "Does Mom sound furious?"

"More upset," I say. "In a hysterical kind of way."

"It's Dad who will be hysterical," Link says.

"No kidding," I say. "This pretty much ruins Christmas."

"This is nothing," Link says. "You haven't seen ruined until they find out I quit Maths for Freaks."

"When did you do that?" I ask. He's been going to Maths for Freaks since forever.

"Ages ago. In September. Almost as soon as I reenrolled."

That's a lot of Saturdays he got up early to run before something he *wasn't* doing started.

"Where have you been going?"

"James didn't tell you?"

"Tell me what?"

"I took over his piano lessons," Link says.

"He didn't exactly tell me," I say, thinking over a few things James did tell me: "He has no clue what he feels about me or math or college" and "You want to keep far away from your brother and math."

"I know he wrote the letter from Dad to Columbia saying you wanted to quit."

"So he did tell you," Link says.

"No, but he wrote a letter from Dad to Cedar Hill so that I could leave the building during lunch."

"I wondered how you guys worked that," Link says. "I

thought you'd be too squeamish to let him fake Dad's signature."

"Oh, no," I say. "It wasn't a problem."

"Obviously."

We stare at each other awkwardly. Complete strangers.

"How's piano going?" I ask.

"Great. Slow. But I'm learning for real. No more goofing around."

I think of all the places—the Wentworths' apartment, the auditorium of my old school, and Cooper's up in Maine—where I have listened to Link goofing around. How can that be no more?

"How do you practice?" I ask, realizing how our not having a piano makes learning for real highly improbable.

"Helena worked it so I can use the practice rooms at Juilliard."

"Is that James's teacher?"

"Yes. She's mine now. She knew I didn't have a piano. All of a sudden."

"You were using James's piano," I say, thinking slowly. "Until you had the fight."

"Yes."

"You had quit Maths for Freaks before you broke up with James."

"I didn't break up with James," Link says, but with weariness. Not as a correction. I force my mind away from who broke up with whom and back onto the piano lessons.

"Mom and Dad aren't going to understand this," I say. "They'll think you should have told them."

"I know what they'll think," Link says. "Which is why I haven't told them."

"Could I hear you play sometime?" I ask, wondering if I will ever know him. If he will ever let me. "If you let people listen, that is. Do you?"

"Helena's having a recital, actually. It's on Sunday. If I'm not executed for treason by our parents, why don't you come?"

"Okay," I say. "What are you playing?"

"A piece by Chopin," he says. "If you come early, before it starts, I'll play 'Edelweiss' for you."

"Edelweiss" is my favorite dumb song from *The Sound of Music*.

"Is there anything I can do?" I ask him. "You know, when they do find out?"

"Lie low," he says. "If they ask, you don't know anything."

"I don't know anything," I say.

"Right," Link says. "Neither do they. I just have to remind them of that."

As if any of us needs reminding. Sometimes we are a family made up of people who know each other, but more and more often we are strangers who occasionally realize we are still living together.

CHAPTER TWELVE

A QUIET BUT PERSISTENT GLOOM INVADES THE APART-
ment. It takes Dad two days to find a flight that will
get him home in time to meet with Cedar Hill's headmaster and the relevant faculty. Mom has to be at one of her
medical offices (for a critical carpet consultation) when
Dad's flight is due in, so she asks Link and me to meet the
plane. Link asks if I would mind staying home.

"They'll make us all sit down as a family after they
hear from the school," my brother says. "I'd like this ini-
tial humiliation to be private."

"Okay," I say. "But it won't be humiliating. Dad will
be like Mom. They only want to know what's going on."

"They are both deeply disappointed," Link says. "It is
a bit hard to bear."

I know exactly what he means, but what was he expecting as he sat for hours without writing in his blue books? As soon as Link leaves for the airport, I go see James. I tell him it's fine that there's nothing to eat except vanilla ice cream. I really want to take a nap.

"Are you sick?" James asks.

"No, tired," I say. "Watching Mom be afraid of Link is harder than smiling at strangers."

I remember my first day at Cedar Hill and how tired and nervous it made me to smile at everyone. I now feel more tired and nervous in my own home.

"It's not so hard to smile at a stranger," James says. "You can do it. I've seen you do it."

"I mean, there's nothing left for Link to do to them," I say, ignoring James's attempt to distract me. I am totally obsessed and worn out by what is and is not happening in my family. "When he told her about Maths for Freaks, she said 'oh.' Like it was the weather."

"Or like it made her too sad to speak," James says. "Give me your sweater. Lie down."

We lie down on his bed, and he reads aloud from *The Little Prince*. In French. I am asleep almost immediately. It's dark out when I wake up. James is reading by the dim light of his bedside lamp.

"What time is it?" I ask, once I know where I am and why.

"It's late," he says. "You really crashed."

"Oh, God," I say. "My parents are going to kill me."

"They think you're staying over at Adena Cohen's house," James says.

"Why do they think that?" I ask him, sitting up and reaching for the bottle of water he keeps by his bed.

"Your brother told them," James says. "He called here about two hours ago. Now, go back to sleep. It's practically midnight."

"You talked to Link?"

"Yes, when he phoned."

"How was it?" I ask. "I mean, how was your conversation?"

"Brief, pleasant. He said to tell you that he was covering for you and not to show up and make him look like a liar."

"He called here for me?" I ask. "I didn't tell Link where I was going."

"I know, but he's not stupid."

"I thought you didn't want him to know about us," I say, remembering the day after Thanksgiving when James wouldn't come to dinner.

"I didn't want him to guess anything that you and I hadn't sorted out first."

"We haven't sorted out so much," I say, thinking of what he says and what we do. How sometimes they match and sometimes they slide past each other.

"Really?"

"I can't sleep here," I say. "I don't have my pajamas. This is your room. Where are your parents?"

Spending the night feels like a boundary that is imperative not to erase. I am in a complete and total panic and pour water down my chin instead of into my mouth.

"Calm down, sweetie. Here, use a glass."

James takes the bottle from my hands and goes into his bathroom, returning with a glass full of water. "You can sleep in your clothes or in a pair of my pajamas. If you want, I'll sleep in the guest room."

"Do your parents know I'm here?"

"No," James says. "They're both in D.C. until the weekend."

"I'm wide awake," I say, getting off the bed, tucking my shirt back inside my skirt. "And I'm starving. I'll go home. I'll tell them I had a fight with Adena."

"Stay," he says. "It would be nice."

"You and I are kind of dating," I say. "My parents would never want me to spend the night here if they knew that. Especially with your parents out of town."

"We're not kind of dating, we're plain dating," James says. "But you're tired and your family is insane right now. Stay."

"No one will believe that we just slept," I say.

"We would," he says.

That's true, we would. And who else is to know, I wonder, before landing on the obvious: Link.

"And your brother did not call here to condone anything we might do," James says. "But to let us both know he was going to trust us."

Link trusts us. I have taken Link's place and he trusts us? If I were Link, would I trust us? Yes, because if I were Link, I would know James very well. Well enough to know that my friend has told my sister that he will not, repeat, not sleep with her.

"I'd love it if the first time I spent the night with a girl it was because she was tired," James says. "I'd love it if it were you."

I sit back down on the bed.

"Will you read me a story?" I ask him. "One in English."

"Pick any story," he says.

"What were you reading while I was asleep?"

"*Mrs. Dalloway*," James says.

"Is it good?"

"It's about a dinner party. It's beautiful, but I'm sure there's no happy ending."

"Read that," I say.

He takes a pair of sweatpants and a flannel shirt from his closet. "I'm going to get you some ice cream with crackers," he says. "Change. You can have all the pillows on your side."

I fold my clothes neatly and put on the flannel shirt. It more than covers my underwear. James's bed has a top sheet and fleece blanket on it. Mom only believes in quilts, as they allow you to make your bed in seven seconds. I slide between the sheets, feeling cool and unusual.

James gives me the ice cream and opens his book. I savor the crush of pillows behind me, the crisp folds around my knees, the sweet smoothness in my mouth, and the sound of James reading about air, vegetables, French windows, and flowers. How could I ever care again that elsewhere people are disappointed, sad, or confused?

CHAPTER THIRTEEN

I GET HOME IN TIME TO GO RUNNING WITH LINK. HE doesn't ask about my night and I don't ask about his. Mom and Dad have already left for the school. It is so cold outside that my chest burns with each breath. We go farther than usual so that by the time I hit the shower, my muscles are thudding instead of feeling bouncy.

"You've gotten really fast," Link says as we poke around the kitchen for something to eat.

There's a nasty smell coming from the vegetable bin. The refrigerator always falls apart when Dad is away. I close its door.

"Let's watch a video," I say as Link carefully peels a too-brown banana and then throws it out.

We go into the living room and I tell Link that I have no desire—none—to watch *That Hamilton Woman*, but that if he wants to see Laurence Olivier in black and white, we can watch *Wuthering Heights*.

"I think not," my brother says. "Stupid movie from a stupid book."

We are not in the mood to venture out and rent anything. We pull *Casablanca* from a box of videos Dad keeps under one of his desks.

"I wonder what's taking them so long," Link says. "They've been gone over three hours."

"They probably went somewhere to have a powwow without us," I say. "To form a strategy."

"Not happening," Link says. "They are nowhere near a united front."

I could have—should have—guessed from Mom's furious, frightened eyes that she was getting ready to blame Dad for what Link has done. No doubt, Dad flew home with a similar intention. I see a much delayed fight taking place about their different ideas regarding my brother's life. I don't see anyone responding to whatever important information Link has put into his blank exams. I hope there will be no yelling involved.

Link and I watch *Casablanca*, standing up to sing along with the actors when Ingrid Bergman's husband tells Humphrey Bogart's band to play the "Marseillaise." Dad taught us the words when we were nine and seven years old.

"This is important," he told us. "No educated person can go to college without knowing this scene by heart."

I think Mom said she managed two years of college just fine without ever having seen *Casablanca*, but perhaps I am imagining a memory. Claude Rains is declaring how shocked he is to discover gambling at Rick's Café when our parents return.

"Kitchen," Mom says. "Five minutes."

I hug Dad. He looks like he could use a seven-hour nap, and I take over at the espresso machine. Mom opens a big red tin of amaretto cookies that she bought on the way home.

"Does she think we're having a party?" Link asks me in a whisper.

We all sit down. This is the drill: The school will let Link take his exams again without putting anything bad on his transcript if he will go into therapy.

"They think it's a behavioral problem," Dad says, setting down his empty espresso cup.

Therapy, which, as far as I know, involves telling someone—a stranger—all your private thoughts. All the things you think in your life but make a point of not saying. I don't see Link going for this. I take Dad's cup and pour more espresso into it. I also give him a glass of water so he won't get the shakes.

"There's nothing wrong with me," Link says. "I'm not going to see a shrink."

"You lied to us," Mom says. "You need someone in your life to whom you can tell the truth."

"I did not lie. I only let you think what you wanted to

think," Link says. "The school should put the grades I've earned on my transcript."

"Exams count for twenty-five percent," Dad says. "You'll have, at best, a straight B minus across the term."

"So?"

"What math department is going to seriously consider you?" Dad asks.

"Colin, that's not what we need to focus on," Mom says.

"I might not do math in college," Link says. "Horror of horrors, I certainly won't apply to Yale."

"At this rate you won't get into any college," Dad says. "Let alone Yale."

"Of course he'll get into a college," Mom says. "Link, let's start at the beginning. What do you want?"

"To be left alone," he says.

"If that's what you truly wanted, you would never have pulled a stunt like this," she says. "I think you would like our attention. It's safe to say you now have it. Is there something you want to tell us?"

"He didn't need to do this to get our attention," Dad says quickly, as if afraid someone else might speak.

"Colin, he sure didn't do it to be left alone," Mom says.

"So why did I do it?" Link asks.

"I have no idea," Mom says. "That's why I'm asking."

"Any ideas?" Link asks, looking at Dad.

"I think you have performance anxiety," Dad says.

This is one of the theories, Mom explains, that the

school raised to justify why Link needs therapy. Math people tend toward the high-strung, they said. They'd always thought Link's outside interests balanced him out, but maybe not enough. An expert would know.

"I do not have performance anxiety," Link says.

"So tell us what's on your mind," Dad says. He could not sound more sarcastic.

"You raised my allowance last month," Link says.

"We did?" Mom asks.

"You didn't raise mine," I say, thinking of all those lunches James had to buy.

"Link had some new expenses," Dad says to me and Mom.

"Untaxed allowance," Link says.

"Untaxed?" Mom asks. "What new expenses?"

Dad is quiet.

"What new expenses?" Mom asks again.

"A girlfriend," Link says, after it's clear Dad isn't going to say anything.

"You gave him a bigger allowance for Polly Keller?" Mom asks.

"I thought he should be equipped for life's inevitable costs," Dad says.

"No, Colin, you didn't." Mom looks devastated. She looks as if no amount of tea or brandy could erase how tired this news has made her. There won't be any yelling. She won't have the energy.

"He did," Link says. "I asked if it was maybe a bribe."

"I remember that. I thought that was strange," Dad says.

"Here's what I remember," Link says. "You said if that's what it took, you were prepared to pay."

What was it like to be Link hearing just how badly Dad wants him to obey those laws that no one will write down? What was it like to be Dad wanting that so badly? I try to look at them as if they are strangers. As if I could ever understand them. I try and I fail.

"Oh, God," Mom says after a fairly hideous silence. "Tell me you didn't say that."

"I might have," Dad says. "But to be fair, one does incur extra expenses by having a girlfriend."

"Oh, God," Mom says again. "Link, I am so sorry."

"Why are you apologizing to him?" Dad asks in a voice as close as his gets to yelling. "He's destroying his future for no reason."

"I think Link has made it abundantly clear why his exams were blank," Mom says. "Do you want him to spell it out for us?"

Right here, captured in this moment, is everything I admire in my mother. Her ability to understand Link and Dad without forcing them to say exactly what they mean. She knows Dad has offered Link money to date a girl instead of James. She knows Link has taken the money and may even want to date Polly instead of James, but is still furious about the offer. Mom can address all this without irrevocably forcing the issue. Good for her.

"I've got nothing to spell out," Link says, sounding much less impressed with her than I am. "Mom, you're overreacting. You both are."

"Fine, but you're going to therapy," Mom says. "Even if I'm the one who is overreacting."

"And you're taking those exams over," Dad says.

"I'm not going to therapy," Link says. "I'm not taking the exams over."

"Let's move on for the moment," Mom says. "Where have you been on Saturday mornings?"

Link tells them about James's piano teacher, Helena.

"I'm studying pretty seriously," Link says. "I like it."

"How can that be serious?" Dad asks. "You don't even have a piano."

"Helena took care of that," Link says. "I practice every day for two hours."

"We could have taken care of it," Mom says. "You could have had lessons if you'd asked."

"You could play piano and do math," Dad says.

"Or just play piano," Mom says.

"Or both," Dad says.

"You have to want to do only math," Link says. "There's no such thing as an outside balance with math. The kind of research, the sort of pure math everyone says I'm good at, I'm not good enough at it."

"You are," Dad says. "Of course you are. You test off the charts. You've just got performance anxiety. You see a shrink for that."

"I'd have to want to," Link says. "I like music. I

always have. I'm not gifted in it. But I like it."

"I see," Dad says, but I can tell he doesn't. He can't.

"There were other ways to handle this," Mom says. "I've always told you it was your choice."

"There were other ways," Link says. "This was the one I chose."

"How impressive," Dad says.

"I'm going out with Ellen now," Link says. "We're going to buy a tree."

"Christmas is in one week," I say, standing up.

"I'll get our coats," Link says and walks out of the kitchen.

"That went even worse than I was dreading," Mom says.

"You should have dreaded more," Dad says.

"I wasn't as informed as you were," Mom says. "Now that I am, be assured that we are finding a shrink not for 'performance anxiety' but for what is real."

"Let's not do this in front of Ellen," Dad says to her.

"Fine, but don't think for a moment that we aren't going to do it."

"We'll get a nice tree," I say, grateful there was no real yelling, but also sort of heartbroken for the two of them. "Everything will settle down."

I must sound a lot less anxious than I feel because they both smile at me. As if I have been reassuring. As if, no matter what else is falling apart, there is me, the one they know and trust.

CHAPTER FOURTEEN

"I HAVE NO DESIRE TO BUY A TREE, ELLEN," LINK SAYS AS soon as we get down to the lobby.

"Um, okay," I say, not surprised, but not thrilled. At some point before Christmas we will need a tree. And we will certainly need a tree in order to return home. To our unhappy and feuding parents. How did this happen? And what, exactly, is it that has happened? No point asking Link, who looks as tired and nervous as Mom and Dad do.

"Is there something else you want to do?" I ask. Anything. Name it. Anything at all.

"No," he says.

"Are you meeting somebody?" I ask.

"No. Sort of. Yes."

"Don't let me keep you," I say.

"You're not keeping me," Link says.

Then what am I doing? Other than standing in the lobby and not buying a tree.

"You want something to eat?" he asks. "I haven't had a peaceful meal since Mom found out."

"Do you have money?"

"Oh, sure," he says. "Untaxed allowance really mounts up."

"So a girlfriend's not as expensive as Dad thought?"

"Not exactly," he says.

It occurs to me that the person who has taught me the most about the art of evasive language and behavior is neither of my skilled parents but my brother. How strange that we should have this crucial bit in common and yet be so different. So separate.

"Where do you want to eat?" I ask him.

"I'm not hungry," he says.

"Link, what is up with you?" I ask, figuring that if we are to do anything, one of us needs to be direct. It works. He stands still and fixes his eyes on me the way Dad does when he's asking if I liked a book and if so, why.

"Did you tell James about my exams?"

"I mentioned it," I say.

"I figured, but he didn't say a thing when I called over there last night."

"He thinks you want him to leave you alone."

"I know what he thinks, but I'm surprised he passed up an opportunity to tell me how thoughtless I am."

This is, in fact, exactly what James said: "Link's

thoughtless as hell. Your parents are going to be wrecked."

"Hmmmm," I say.

"Here's the thing, I'd like to see him," Link says. "I have this idea that if we can get together, you know, the three of us, it will iron itself out."

Right. As if James were anything like Mom. As if James will let Link back without irrevocably forcing every issue under the sun. But he might. I don't know what it would mean for me, but I don't want to be with James if he'd rather have Link. Not true: I want to be with James no matter whom he loves more. Except that I would feel yucky, I would feel second best being with James if he wanted Link back. If they can deal with each other, they should have a fresh chance to choose.

"Well, if you want to see him, you should call him," I say.

"Could you call him?" Link asks. "I don't know if he wants to see me, but he'll do it as a favor to you."

As a favor to me. I suppose this is as close as we will come to discussing the current shift between the three of us. Link and I find a working pay phone on Columbus and Seventy-second Street. He hands me enough change to talk for over an hour.

"I'm going across the street," he says. "For privacy and decorum's sake."

And so I can say whatever I need to say to get James to come with us.

"How are you?" I ask all cheery bright when he picks up the phone.

"Exhausted," he says. "You are a cover hog."

This is James's idea of a joke, as he slept with his arms around me but on top of the covers I was tucked into.

"Link wants to see you," I say, not laughing. I outline what I think has come to pass with school, therapy, exams, Polly, and money. "He won't take his exams over. Or see a shrink. But he wants me to ask you to come eat with us. Please come."

"You're having a bad day," James says.

"Oh, no, this has been so good," I tell him. "My parents probably need therapy more than Link. They think I'm out buying a Christmas tree and spent last night with Adena because I don't lie to them. Why would I be having a bad day?"

"Give me half an hour to get showered and dressed, okay?"

"Okay," I say. "Thank you." By the way, what kind of day are you having? Was it as nice as you thought to sleep with a girl who was tired?

We meet at James's favorite restaurant over on Second Avenue. He and my brother eat hamburgers and drink beer and . . . well, they catch up. They each hated one of the novels they had to read in English class (a book by Thomas Hardy, which I resolve to read immediately), but for different reasons. They thought the same thing when they cut into their lab frogs for biology: It's freakishly dry inside this creature. But there's just so much of school they can discuss without bumping into topics they want to avoid. So after a review of their classes with no mention of their exams, they fall silent.

"I finally finished *Tale of Two Cities*," Link says after a while. "I liked it, but you were right. She was not worth dying for."

"You reading anything else?" James asks.

"No," Link says. "Between track and piano, I barely have time to breathe."

James asks how the piano lessons are going. "Ellen says you're playing Chopin. Is it the E-flat Nocturne?"

"The very one," Link says. "Helena said it was what made you quit."

"Listening to you play it after hearing it once made me quit," James says.

"Well, now I play it with my fingers in all the right places," Link says. "She had me do scales nonstop for two months. It was horrible."

"You're kidding," James says. "Helena used to say there was no point in perfect technique if I didn't feel the music."

"She tells me there's no point in playing music if I can't execute it properly."

They laugh. If it weren't for James's knee leaning deliberately against mine, it would be like old times.

"Why don't you come?" Link asks. "To the recital. Come with Ellen."

"You should ask your parents," James says.

"I should ask them both to go to hell," Link says.

I am really surprised to hear him use the word *hell*. Swearing is not allowed at home. Dad says it is the product of a limited mind. That we are not thinking with intelligence if we resort to swearing. It's one of his mind and its heartbeat rules.

"For what?" James asks.

"For thinking they know so much," Link says.

"They know what you tell them," James says.

"They think they know more," Link says.

"Like what?" James asks.

My brother shrugs. "Just stuff."

"Let me guess," James asks. "They're still afraid you're gay."

So that's what it is. Fear. Dad's afraid Link's gay, and Mom's afraid Dad will be or already is handling it badly. It's not that either of them *knows*. They can't *know* anything for sure about Link. But the fear is everywhere. I do admire Mom, but I love James for saying clearly and fearlessly what is going on. I look to Link, who does not love clear and fearless speech nearly as much.

"Yeah, pretty much," he says. "They still are. Pretty much afraid."

"Well, they will stay afraid as long you do."

"I am not gay," Link says, a familiar weariness in his voice.

"I know," James says. "We've all seen the girl. Well done. Ask her to the recital."

"She doesn't like classical music," Link says. "And

she's afraid of you. So she won't come if you're there."

"Really," says James. He could not sound more pleased.

"She thinks your opinion carries a lot of weight with me," Link says. "Which is funny. Dad thinks the exact same thing, and they could not be more different. Imagine my father thinking just like Polly Keller."

"Your father means well," James says. "And when you want to tell him what he is afraid to know, he might find a way to approve."

"I tried to talk to Dad," Link says. "But it was pointless. It wouldn't change what he thinks is best."

"It doesn't matter what he thinks is best," James says. "It's what you think."

"Right," Link says. "What I think matters to him."

"You matter to him," James says. "You underestimate what that is worth."

I know that Mr. Wentworth is almost never home. And once a week Mrs. Wentworth calls James from her office to schedule dinner with him. It's usually on a Tuesday when Mr. Wentworth has dinner with the senior partners. It's impossible to imagine Mr. Wentworth as interested in or preoccupied with James as Dad is with us.

"I matter less than what he thinks is important," Link says. "And what could I have told him?"

"Whatever you were thinking," James says. "The truth."

"What could I have told him that was true?" Link

asks. "What is there about me that's true, and is it anything he wants to know?"

I see my brother now as I failed to earlier. The discussion about allowances and bribes would have taken place in Dad's study. Link's face comes into focus against the disorderly shelves. He is sad and furious at what he is being told. At realizing that what he has been unable to say to James and me might, in fact, be true. I suddenly understand just how many hours of exams I could sit through not writing but thinking of my father's offer to pay money for that particular truth to become a lie.

"You could have told him whatever you are telling yourself," James says.

"I don't think that would have helped much," Link says. "Which is, I realize, your point."

"I don't have a point," James says. "Other than your father will stay afraid only for as long as you allow it."

"I'll invite my parents to the recital," Link says. "You've convinced me."

He sounds very unconvinced.

"They'll like that," I say.

"Will you come?" Link asks James.

"Yes."

I watch expressions rush into Link's face, which make it mysterious and beautiful. He is shy, thrilled, delighted, furious, ashamed, and frightened. Maybe he's not gay, but he loves James. I wish that loving James made Link as happy as it makes me. I wish I knew why it didn't. I look at

Link's newly mysterious and beautiful face and think, *There's nothing I wouldn't do for you.*

Perhaps I love Link more than I can imagine loving James. More than Mr. Rochester loved Jane. The question that presents itself is what am I going to do about it? I am learning how to love James. Can I learn how best to love my brother?

"Thanks," Link says to James's yes.

When the check arrives, Link insists on paying. I ask him if he feels like buying a tree yet.

"Oh, the tree," Link says. "We're so not ready for Christmas this year. What happened?"

I know what he means. Usually we go ice skating at Rockefeller Center with Mom and have hot chocolate at Rumplemeyer's with Dad. My old school had a Christmas pageant on the second Sunday in December, with the students playing all the parts from the Nativity. I was always a shepherd or a sheep until last year, when I was Gabriel. It totally cracked Link and James up that I had this horrible stage fright and my lines started with, "Fear not, Mary: for thou hast found favor with God."

This year, on the second Sunday in December, I was at Kennedy Airport with James. We were celebrating the end of exams. He was drawing and I was reading his copy of Vasari's *Lives of the Artists*. Christmas was the last thing on my mind.

"Have either of you bought even one present?" James asks.

"I got Helena a scarf," Link says. "But nothing for anybody else."

"You guys better get busy," James says.

Link thinks he and I should go back to the West Side to buy the tree, as no one on the East Side is going to deliver crosstown.

"Call me later," James says, and I look at Link to see if he will before realizing that the request is directed at me.

"See you on Sunday, then, if you can," Link says.

"Looking forward to it," James says.

They stand on either side of the table, putting coats and scarves on. There is a formality in their words, a stiffness in their bodies that I can only see because I have never seen it before. I wonder if without me—without their useless insurance—they would shed their new armor. If I could make this happen, would it be the right way to love Link or just the wrong way to love James?

CHAPTER FIFTEEN

I T TAKES A FEW DAYS FOR MOM AND DAD TO FIND THEIR way to a united front. During that time we perform the rituals that make up our idea of Christmas. We decorate the tree, buy and wrap presents, eat everything Dad cooks, and help Mom hang up the fifty-seven cards that arrive from people with too much time on their hands.

They both come to the recital, which is incredibly boring. Mom hugs James; Dad's eyes look elsewhere as he shakes James's hand. Link is the only student who plays with no sheet music and without any obvious mistakes.

"So much for performance anxiety," Mom says to Dad as the polite clapping of anxious parents dies down.

"United front" is perhaps an overstatement; it's more like bandaged fragments. Without any warning, the dinner hour (which suddenly reemerges the night of the recital) morphs into a family meeting. This is the new drill: Link is sixteen years old and lives at home. They respect his maturity and growing autonomy, but in the end, as long as he lives under their roof, he will comply with their authority. He will see a shrink.

"You can do as you please with your exams," Mom says. "But you cannot do as you please with your life. Not while I still have a say in it."

"You can make me go," Link says, "but you can't force me to talk to anyone. It's a waste."

"Your persistent retreat into silence is precisely why you are going into therapy," Mom says.

"What, all of a sudden silence in this house is a bad thing?" Link asks. "When the hell did this happen?"

"Your language is unnecessary," Dad says.

"Va te faire foutre," Link says slowly, his accent impeccable.

Those are the first words I learned in French. James and Link taught them to me. They are not printable in family newspapers.

"Damn it to hell, Link," Mom says, and I think, wow, Mom's lost it. Totally lost it. I have never heard her say *damn*. Even when she breaks something. This is just great. My whole family's going to hell. I should probably say this aloud. Join in the fun.

"Apologize to your father," Mom says.

"No," Dad says. "Let's just move on."

"To what?" Mom asks. It's a question she directs at no one in particular.

"The silent therapy," Link says.

"I'd like some tea," Mom says, and I move toward the stove, stopping at the sink to fill the kettle.

"I need a drink," Dad says, leaving the kitchen.

He comes back with two cognac snifters filled a quarter of the way up. He gives one to Mom, who puts it next to the teacup and saucer I have set out for her. We all sit, waiting for the water to boil. We sit as if the whistle of steam will erase the sound of Link swearing at Dad in French. It might. I turn the kettle off and bring a pot of tea to the table. It almost works. I can hardly imagine that it has happened.

"There is nothing wrong with silence," Mom says, pouring her tea with one hand, holding her drink with the other. "It's not a bad way to express yourself. What concerns us about your silence is that you are not sure what you are expressing with it."

"I'm sure," Link says. "I know what I am expressing."

"I'm not convinced you do," Mom says. "It's a bit too loud for you to be so certain."

"What will it take for you to believe I know what my silence means?" Link asks.

"When it's not so hostile," Mom says. "I don't mind the hostility aimed at us, but so much of it is landing on you."

"Okay, you have a deal," my brother says after burying his head in his hands as a gesture of mock horror and defeat. "I'm not taking my exams over. I want that particular piece of hostility to stay on the table. But I'll see a shrink."

"Yeah, you will," Dad says.

"I suppose you've picked somebody out," Link says.

"We have a list of names," Mom says. "We are open to suggestions."

"There was a girl from when I was in ninth grade," Link says. "At Maths for Freaks."

"Accelerated Math for the Advanced Student," Dad says, using the proper name for Columbia's math program.

"Colin," Mom says. It is a warning. It is a plea. It is so far away from his name. "We know what he means."

Link says that the girl had a total breakdown. Weighed about seventy-eight pounds, and when that didn't kill her, she tried pills and a blade. She had to take a year off from school. She wound up seeing a doctor in Princeton. A doctor famous for working with high-strung math kids. As far as I'm concerned, this should be Dad's sole Christmas present: to know that the heartbeat inside Link's mind might still consist of numbers and their equations.

Over the break, I make every effort to maneuver Link into coming with me when I go out with James. My brother slips away each time, without letting me know if he doesn't want to see James, doesn't want to see James with me around, or is just, as he says, busy. We continue to talk around what is different in our lives in relation to James. I continue to have no idea of who Link is. What he thinks. What he might want from James. Or from me.

So I go to work on a different target. Surely James will

take advantage of chances that Link keeps turning down. James's father gives him two tickets for New Year's Day at Carnegie Hall. The Philadelphia Orchestra is playing an all-Strauss program.

"Traditional New Year's music, mostly," James says. "Waltzes. Do you want to come?"

Of course I do, but I ask James if he wouldn't rather take Link.

"No," James says.

"But it's music," I say. "Link is good at music."

"But it's my afternoon and my tickets," James says. "I'd prefer to go with you."

"I want you to ask Link," I say, resorting to the truth.

"Ellen, if you don't want to go, just say so. My dad can give these to any number of people."

"I want you to spend some time with Link," I say. "Alone. Without me."

"Don't you think it would make more sense if that happened because it was something he and I wanted?"

"Isn't it something you want?" I ask.

"Not particularly," James says. "And it's not something he wants. But if either of us did, I could see him and still take you to the concert."

He's right. When and if they need to see each other, they won't need me to arrange it.

"So are you coming or not?" James asks.

"Yes," I say. "Thank you."

I wind up having a lot to thank him for, as the music

is joyful and elegant and it makes me feel as if the New Year will bring me nothing but joy and elegance. I picture its unfolding as a huge piece of Steuben glass full of diffused light and solid weight.

CHAPTER SIXTEEN

B EFORE SCHOOL RESUMES, DAD GETS AROUND TO MY irrelevant grades. We are having lunch at a new place on Spring Street. Dad came here with the money people at his office, and now he wants to check it out when he can really appreciate the food. I order something with the words *roasted, julienne,* and *petals* in it. Whenever I go out to eat with my father, I always wish I were a menu writer.

"I've noticed you're reading *Tess of the d'Urbervilles,*" Dad says. "How are you finding it?"

Tess of the d'Urbervilles is the novel by Thomas Hardy which James and Link hated. It is totally incomprehensible. So far, Tess has been raped, married, and abandoned. In order to know as little as that, I have had to read almost every page twice. In addition to laying out his plot, Hardy is busy making points about religion, politics, and class warfare. I don't know what the points are. Just that they are being made and I am missing them.

"The book has its rewards," I say, which is not a lie. I don't like reading it, but an unmistakable self-satisfaction occurs every time I figure out the plot.

"A girl capable of reading Hardy is capable of doing much better than you did in English," Dad says.

Here it comes, I think. Be brave. You got bad grades. Now justify them. Show him who you truly are.

"Algebra, I can understand," Dad continues, granting me a minor break before getting down to business. "Even chemistry, although if you give yourself a chance, you will find the world there. French is a matter of discipline, which can come and go at your age. English, however, involves reading and thinking. Two things I know you to be totally in command of."

There is a compliment tucked inside this accounting of my failures, and so I step into the shell of the girl he knows.

"I was distracted," I say pleasantly. "I'll do better next semester."

"Distracted is what happened to you in French, in chemistry, and in algebra," Dad says. "But there's no excusing your English grade. How does one get distracted from thinking?"

No excusing your English grade? He's being ridiculous, and I resolve to bring us both onto a more reasonable playing field.

"One gets distracted by thinking of other things," I

say. "My English teacher spent the whole semester making us read books and plays that she never wanted to discuss properly. Thinking for her was a waste of time."

Dad asks for examples, and I give him a little tirade about reading *Ethan Frome* and then never talking about repressed sexual desire. The absurdity of reading *The Crucible* and acting like it can only be about Communists in the 1950s.

"It *is* about Communists in the 1950s," Dad says as if he is going to have to explain McCarthyism to me.

"That's how it was written," I say, "but there's no reason why it can't be read with the plight of gay people coming to mind."

Did I really use the word *plight*? If James thinks the word *pretentious* accurately describes the things he says, a whole new adjective will have to be created for me.

"Couldn't you have thought about Communists for the test and about gay people on your own time?" Dad asks.

"Yes, but I can't make myself think about things that aren't interesting," I say. "Of course I have the ability, but I don't know that I'm going to use it as often as you wish I would."

"Okay," he says. "That's fair."

"Fair has nothing to do with it," I say, so that we're clear. "It's more to do with the type of person I am."

With the quality of my mind's particular heartbeat.

"You will lose out on a lot of things if you don't force

yourself to learn beyond your own interests," Dad says, "but I believe you already understand that."

Over huge plates of flourless chocolate cake, he asks, cautiously, if he may know what I have been thinking about in lieu of my schoolwork. That's easy: James and Link. Link and James. James. Link. James. James. Sex. James. James. Link. Even I am bored by this answer, and so I give my father a better, cleaner one.

"How to see," I say, explaining about hospitals, airports, lists of what people might own, and the fact that girls have interesting qualities. "It's a way to understand somebody you will never know."

Dad listens to me. Absorbs me, really. His eyes never leave my face, and I picture my words piercing through his corneas down into his heart. I am reminded of why Link and I want his attention even when we dread it. We want it because when we don't disappoint Dad, we present him with our best selves.

I talk about how Michelangelo was gay, and isn't that ironic, given that he also designed the Vatican, which is where the Pope lives. The Pope, who has to make gay people feel bad as part of his job. I say that reading about art and gay people at the same time has been really interesting. So many really good artists and writers and dancers are gay. I have to wonder why that is.

"I've often wondered the same thing myself," Dad says. "But I've never come up with an answer that transcends the obvious."

We have arrived, quite by accident, at a discussion about gay people. Perhaps this is a talk that belongs to my brother. It also, however, belongs to me. If my family is going to hell because Link is gay, I have the right to know why.

"What is the obvious?" I ask. "About artists and gay people?"

"Margins," Dad says. "Perspective."

"Could you be more specific?" I ask. James would be proud.

"Like most minorities, gay people are forced to live outside the mainstream of society," Dad says.

"That's ridiculous," I say. "Lots of famous people are gay." Of course, right at this moment the only famous gay people I can think of are dead.

"Famous is not the issue," Dad says. "It's that by virtue of being different from the majority, gay people find themselves outside. In life's margins, if you will. From there, they are able to make unique observations. Most art—dance, music, poetry, what have you—is an expressed observation."

I consider this information slowly. Perhaps my father is not so clueless after all. It's only by being forced to navigate (as opposed to simply obeying) society's unwritten laws that you realize they exist. And that allows you—forces you—to look at things differently from the way people who follow the laws without much, if any, thought look at things.

"What makes you care so much about Link?" I ask.

"Don't you want him to have a unique perspective?"

"Your brother is not gay," Dad says.

"We don't know that," I say, thinking how the more I hear Dad and Link say he is not gay, the less I believe it. "He doesn't even know. You're afraid he is. Why?"

"Link is endlessly talented," Dad says. "He's crawling with potential. While the margins may afford certain observations, it is also a limited way to live. I want your brother's life to be limitless."

"It could be limitless either way," I say. "I think it's wrong of you to care. It's worse than wrong. It's stupid."

"Oh, my," Dad says. He is kind of smiling. "I see."

I am as exhausted and exhilarated as someone who has just finished an extralong, extrafast run. We are having a disagreement, and I am not going to either yell at or disappoint my father. Amazing.

"You don't see," I say. "If you did, you'd let Link know it doesn't matter."

"It does matter," Dad says. "It matters to me. And I believe that Link and I have let each other know as much as we need to about the topic."

"You've both *not* let each other know things," I say.

"Give me some credit, Ellen," Dad says. "If Link were convinced that James were right for him, no amount of money in the world could have kept Polly around. Let me have my peace while your brother remains undecided."

I am so startled to hear the truth—the clear and fearless truth—from my father, of all people, that I don't say anything.

125

"Now, should it ever come to pass that you want to sleep with a girl, we can pursue this conversation further. But for now, I am done."

"I don't want to sleep with a girl," I say. "I love James."

This is why no one in my family ever says anything. Look at the way private—totally and irrevocably private—things just slip out.

"I mean, not really," I amend hastily. "I just think so."

"This vacillating affection appears to run in the family," Dad says, signaling for the check.

Okay, fine. It's all fine. He is going to pretend that he didn't hear anything important or private. Just as I am going to pretend that I didn't say anything about sex and James in front of my father.

On the way home, we stop at a stationery supply store on West Tenth Street. Dad would like to buy me a sketch-pad. And pencils of my choosing.

"I'm interested," he says, "to see what you see."

"I can't draw," I say.

"Do we know that for sure?" he asks.

I pick out a pad with heavy white paper that tears out along perforated edges, a charcoal pencil just like the kind James uses, and a set of colored ones imported from Switzerland. I take a long time making my selections, as if they are of the utmost importance. There is very little of which I know for sure, and the chance to discover a talent is not an opportunity to rush past.

CHAPTER SEVENTEEN

I COVER PAGE AFTER PAGE. I DRAW EVERY ROOM OF THE house in Maine. Link's model airplanes in their various stages of being built. The kitchen right at the start of a dinner party for Important Guests. Mom and Dad in the living room after Important Guests have left. I do blown-up detail drawings of Mom's tea trays, Link's immaculate desk, and the unruly stacks of Dad's cookbooks.

Images creep up on me the way smoke from James's cigarettes eventually drifts my way. In my mind, I see whatever makes itself clear, and I let it out through the pencil and onto the paper. I can do this. Here's what I can't do: draw anything I'm looking at. If I look right at Mom, her laptop, or Dad's espresso machine, my fingers turn thick and clumsy.

I bring my new pencils, the pad, and my drawings—

both the ones I like and the ones I can't finish—to James for advice and instruction.

"When did you start this?" James asks, his hands and attention moving from my face to my drawings.

"It was Dad," I say.

I tell him about lunch. Almost all of it: Thomas Hardy, my grades, chocolate cake, and what Dad said about gay people and artists.

"It's a valid point of view," James says, and then, "Some of these are really good, Ellen."

He keeps looking through the drawings. The word *some* makes me nervous, and without exactly meaning to I blurt out how Dad said that Link didn't think James was right for him.

"He said that's why Link took the money," I say. "That if Link were more sure about you, he would have refused it."

"Again, that's a valid point of view," James says, putting my things down. "It's also a very convenient opinion for him to have."

"What do you mean, 'convenient'?" I ask, distressed that my drawings are now lying on the bed between us. I wonder which ones belong to *some*.

"Your father doesn't want to think Link chose Polly to please him," James says. "He wants to think that the 'undecided' is in some way true. How else will it bring him any peace?"

"But it is true," I say, clearly recalling my father's face

and voice at lunch. "I mean, Dad wasn't lying to me. He believes that Link would never have dated Polly if he had really loved you."

"Of course he wasn't lying," James says. "I'm not calling your father a liar. He told you what he thinks is true."

"He believes a lie?" I ask, knowing that this is exactly what James means. Dad already believes what he hopes Link will: He didn't love James enough to defy Dad's wishes. To my father *enough* is what divides gay love from straight.

"He believes the truth he wants to," James says. "It might be the truth Link believes as well. It's not important."

His hands move through my drawings, dividing them into two piles.

"Ellen, sweetie, look at how amazing some of these are. These are important."

"Define *some*," I say, and he does.

I'm right that the drawings I do from memory are the good ones. James thinks I get a form of stage fright when I try to record what I see. I will improve. In the meantime, look at the way I have failed to make the teacup smaller than the pot. Look at how Link's different airplane parts look too much alike. Do it over. Be precise. Be clear.

I do and I am.

I show my drawings to everyone. I am not secretive with them the way James is with his. I don't see the point. He doesn't like to think that another pair of eyes will spot an error before he does, but I feel just the opposite. Only another pair of eyes will see what I have missed. He shrugs. And I tell him that, of course, it's different for me. I am nowhere near as good as he is. In the few drawings James lets me see, there is a spirit. It's like they are alive. Mine are recordings of what I dredge up from my memory and my imagination. Precise and clear recordings, but in no way alive.

"Not yet," James says a few days later, after another review.

From a glass-encased bookshelf in his parents' guest room, he gives me books with illustrations by Beatrix Potter, Kate Greenaway, Mary Shepard, and Ludwig Bemelmans, whose drawings you can see in the Bemelmans Bar at the Carlyle Hotel. James says not to get distracted by the colors. To follow the lines. The lines are what matters.

Arranged correctly, lines make lamplight, plaid skirts, bangs, thin noses, and large eyes. If once upon a time I would have followed James to the moon and Link anywhere, today I am only prepared to follow a line. To crack its code as it makes drawings that are alive.

School starts, and I tolerate its many intrusions upon my life as best I can. I never do finish the book by Thomas Hardy. I put it down after Tess falls back in love with the man who has previously abandoned her. I will read this book again when I can either understand or bring myself to care about Hardy's points. Except for

French and chemistry (my father may be right about finding the world there and how will I know if I don't pay precise and clear attention?), my grades do not improve significantly.

I feel less concerned about attention. You can hardly hand your drawings out, asking for feedback, and not expect—not want—attention in one form or another. I do a drawing of Adena in the courtyard, but dressed up as if she were the Queen of England. For Laurel, I do one of her talking on the phone while painting her toenails.

They are easier to be around, now that avoiding them isn't a top priority. Learning to look at people—to imagine who they are, what they own, and why—has given me an ability to endure the possibility that I am being looked at. Each morning at assembly, Adena and Laurel ask to see my sketchpad and flip through it, looking for new drawings and where, on old ones, James has made fresh corrections.

"I do not correct," he says. "I make suggestions. If you take them, they become part of your drawing and therefore your idea."

There are times when James reminds me much too much of Dad, and I wonder if Link ever noticed this. Of course, I don't ask. My brother has started therapy, heading to New Jersey two afternoons a week. The doctor in Princeton agreed to take Link on only after talking with the headmaster, the director of Maths for Freaks, and an outside specialist who gave Link what amounted to a five-hour math exam. The doctor is named Anthony Koch and does not, he told Mom and Dad, like to fail his patients.

"So I go the extra distance to ensure that we're a good match," he said.

"He goes the extra distance to see if I'm smart enough to crack up," Link said. "Dr. Koch doesn't like ordinary screwups."

God forbid Link should be an ordinary screwup. I'd love it if by seeing Dr. Koch, my brother became more ordinary. Someone who leaves arguments without shattering glass. Someone capable of speaking in a clear and fearless manner. Not all the time, of course. That would be crazy, in my family. But when different ideas—different truths—collide, nothing is helped by silence. Not in my family.

So far all Dr. Koch has done is suggest that Link quit track and start tutoring. Not math students, mind you, but third graders. And not, as Mom assumed, third graders in the public school system. Regular third graders in our school who need a little extra help during the three afternoons a week Link isn't with Dr. Koch.

I see my brother less often now because we don't run together anymore. When I do see him—at dinner, outside Dad's study, or the glimpse here and there at school—he is as moody and secretive as ever. This is where only being able to draw from memory and imagination (as opposed to, you know, reality) comes in handy. My sketchbooks are full of drawings of Link. Link asleep on the porch in Maine. Link in the school courtyard. Link in my room, perched on my desk, surveying the mess with disdain.

Link never even passes through my room, but through my pencils he goes anyplace I want him to. Unlike James, who is much harder to draw than Link. In my drawings, James often winds up looking like my brother.

"It's the mouth," James says. "We do basically look alike except for that."

And the truth is they do look basically the same. I never thought that they looked different until after I had fallen *totally madly in love* with James.

"But your eyes," I say, wanting to draw them as distinct, and frustrated that I can't. "Your eyes are different."

"Yes, but you've figured that out."

Sort of. I was looking at the different lines their noses needed when I noticed that Link's eyes are close to his nose whereas James's are more widely spaced. Their mouths remain beyond my talents. Which is a drag, as mouths matter a lot more than you might think. Much more than eyes. I think we expect eyes to reveal by being guarded or tearful or bright. But it's the mouth that holds the key to any expression.

Aside from Link, I prefer places to people as drawing subjects: houses, gardens, parks, views, and rooms. Dad's study is my favorite. Probably because it has looked so different over the years that when I summon it up, it is never the same. No one drawing of Dad's study looks like another until I think to include one of the volumes of the three-volume novel in German.

Der Mann ohne Eigenschaften. The Man Without Qualities by Robert Musil. It is easy enough to put a thick book, which I color in red, anywhere I please in every version of the study. The book serves as a thread that sews all the different studies into one.

"What is this about?" I ask Dad one night, picking up volume two. It is so long I cannot imagine that there is an end that can be described as either happy or true.

"A lost world," he says. "A life just out of reach."

This is fitting, since I think his finishing it will remain forever out of reach. I would venture that its length and difficulty are why he is reading it in the first place. But of course I don't know if that is, in fact, true. Dad learned French, Latin, and Italian in college, but he taught himself German. Was it to read this book? Why not read a three-volume book in French? I leave the study. Suppose he answered all my questions. I still wouldn't discover what the quality is of *his* mind's heartbeat. Which is what I am really asking with my questions about his reading habits.

And yet . . . how could he possibly answer me? Really answer, I mean. He is my father, and maybe you aren't supposed to know family the way you know other people. Not that I think I know other people. Do I know James so much better than I know Link, or do I only have more access to James? Perhaps there are limits to how much you can know anyone, an unwritten social law that I am in the process of learning. Somebody should write these things down.

CHAPTER EIGHTEEN

JAMES AND I HAVE BECOME AN ITEM AT CEDAR HILL.
Much the same way Link and Polly are. James finds the
comparison ridiculous but inevitable. We have stopped
fleeing the cafeteria at lunch, and when last period ends,
James waits for me by my locker so that we can walk to his
house together. I have the distinct impression that this
simple change in my schedule has convinced Laurel and
Adena that I am no longer a virgin.

If I were not afraid of Adena and what I envision she
knows, I would pull her aside and ask if it is normal to be
in love with someone who has made up his mind that sex
will not happen. Not, repeat, not. I would ask her if I
missed the class when they explained love and sex. Was I
reading through that bit? How else would I know so little
about what makes the body—mine and his—tremble, leak,

and break open? How can there be no written laws—none at all—about how to love someone? And how come the only laws I can find written down about how to have sex concern not getting pregnant or caught or dead?

I don't ask Adena. I let her think what she will. I don't ask anyone and find that I am, once again, in the process of flying blind as I learn. Whenever I stray for too long on James's body, he will say "Ellen" as a warning and a plea. It makes me think of my parents, which makes me stop doing whatever I am doing.

So some things happen and some don't. The things that happen are good, and I believe that more would be better. James thinks that when it comes to sex, less is more. And then, there's the little matter of an AIDS test. He keeps meaning to have one.

When we close the door to his room, James always looks at my hands, checking them for paper cuts or hang nails. It seems we have read the exact same safe-sex manuals, the detailed ones about blood and bodily fluids and the insignificant turning deadly. I like James's somewhat clinical ritual at the start of our *not* having sex. After all, you can never be too careful. Especially since he himself hasn't always been. Sometimes, when we are lying in bed, done with whatever is going to happen, he will say, "You are only fourteen."

As if it explains his reluctance and unease with where I very much want us to go. Think we should go. Now, when we are wrapped up in each other's lives. Waiting for me to get past fourteen is like waiting for us to unravel. I might not want to in another year.

There is also the way sex is like drawing for me. When I touch James or when I pick up my pencil, I want to keep going until it is finished. I have a clearer idea of what sex looks like finished than of what a drawing does, but the feeling of being pulled into another place is the same in sex and with drawing.

"You'll go to college," I finally reply to James's announcement of my age. "There will be someone else, and waiting will have been silly."

It is the last day of February, which lasts a long time for such a short month. Colleges will send out acceptances and rejections in less than two months.

"You're as likely to have someone else as I am," he says.

"All the more reason," I say. "I don't want the first time to be with someone who isn't you."

"I don't want your first time to be with someone who has never been with a girl," James says, speaking more to the ceiling than to me. "And that would be who I am right now."

I think it is the men he has been with that make James reluctant. The men he slept with in order to annoy Link. I read in one of my books on gay identity (or was it in yet another good-sex-is-safe-sex pamphlet?) that when you have sex with someone, you have sex with all the people that person has slept with. Perhaps James is some-what creeped out by the idea of those men coming into

137

contact with me when they were meant to help him reach my brother.

I don't know. It's very confusing. I ask James if he thinks I would prefer his sleeping with another girl—a woman (surely a girl in college is a woman)—before he sleeps with me.

"I would certainly prefer it," he says.

"Men are strange," I say, repeating something I have read in many, many places.

"They sure are," James says. "You have no idea."

And we laugh. Because it is funny. The picture of us I will draw later. The one of me and James in bed with the three men he has slept with. I was right about the waiter in Maine and the senior from school who is now at Emory.

The first time was with a friend—a protégé, really, an up-and-comer at the law firm—of Mr. Wentworth's. The friend/protégé is the one James was not careful with. He is the one James's shrink thinks had nothing to do with Link and everything to do with Mr. Wentworth. James refers to this man as The Weapon.

"If I were to tell my father," James says, "it would be as bad as if I shot him."

The Weapon is named Douglas Peters, and when James was only fifteen he was able to leave the impression that he was from Mr. Wentworth's first marriage.

"I would have needed to be at least twenty-eight to be as old as the Coven," James says. "But I don't think he was doing math really well. He figured I was out of college. Old enough to hit on."

Douglas Peters cried when he found out how old James really was. James says he doesn't know if the tears were from fear or grief.

"Probably both," I say.

Link was, James tells me, furious when he found out.

"Your brother thought this was all the proof he needed that I could not be trusted," James says. "It made him afraid."

"Did you want it to?" I ask.

"I don't know," James says. "I thought we would talk it over and figure out what had happened."

"You thought my brother would talk to you about your having had sex?" I ask. "With another person? With a man?"

"I did think so, yes," James says, laughing. "But I was quickly set straight."

"So to speak," I say, turning over the possibility that Douglas Peters had made Link afraid. "Had he trusted you before?"

"Not like you do," James says. "Not really ever. I used to believe that things I had done were what kept Link and me apart, but now I just think it was the wrong time for us."

"Sort of like it was the wrong time for you and Douglas Peters?" I ask. "If you had met him when you were older, he wouldn't have cried."

"If I'd been older, I wouldn't have slept with him," James says. "By now, I have other ways to deal with my father. Less fear inducing ones."

"I'm not afraid," I say, holding out my hand for his.

I am only fascinated and try to think if Dad has any friends Link or I would sleep with. It is impossible to imagine. The Weapon makes me more jealous than afraid. He is the best part of the drawing, which turns out to be not in a bedroom but in a waiting room. The kind you find at a doctor's office. Of the five of us—James, the other men, and me—who are waiting it is Douglas Peters, whom I have never met or seen, who looks most like a person. He is the only one with an expression. The only one whose mouth I got just right so that his face is full of sorrow instead of merely frozen, the way my fingers still are if I try to draw what I see.

CHAPTER NINETEEN

D R. KOCH ARRANGES FOR LINK TO TAKE ANOTHER
exam. This one in French. The results confirm what
they have guessed after conducting four of their sessions
in French. With only three and a half years of high school
French, Link has become fluent.

"He wants to see how fast I can teach myself Latin,"
Link says.

"I can help you," Dad says. "I still have all my books
from college."

Dad has what he calls a working grasp of French. He
is not fluent. I don't think he is overjoyed with Link's
newly discovered talent.

"I have to teach myself," Link says. "It's the whole
point of the exercise. The French was an accident. He
wants to see what happens when I apply myself."

"How will he determine that you are fluent in Latin?" Dad asks.

"When I can translate it into Greek," Link says. "And back again. You know, the way a certain kind of boy can."

There's a huge relationship between Greece and gay people. I'm not exactly sure what it is, but it appears to be common knowledge and to have something to do with Socrates, whose life I studied in the seventh grade and have since forgotten. The word *Hellenic* comes up all the time in books by gay men. It seems really clear to me from Link's tone of voice and his piercing look that he's telling Dad something about himself that has nothing to do with language skills.

"I see" is all Dad says.

"I see" is how Dad stays in conversations without actually taking part in them. If I were Dad, I wouldn't even stay in a conversation with Link these days. Link doesn't say much, but when he does it is as if he is issuing a dare. Sometimes the dare is about his academic future or his potential math career. But more and more often the dare is about his future sex life.

If I were honest, I would say that my brother's unpredictable willingness to hint that he is gay is the main reason behind my hurry to sleep with James. But I am not particularly overcome with the need to be honest about sex and James. It's too confusing.

"Dr. Koch wants you to learn Greek?" Mom asks Link.

This is her way of staying in conversations with Link—by taking his dares and hints at face value. It is as if she is daring him back to say what he means.

"He hasn't said anything about learning Greek," Link says. "But I might. Almost every aspect of civilization can be traced back to Ancient Greece. Greek would have its uses. In lots of areas. Not all academic."

Again the knowing, I-dare-you tone of voice and the look. I need to get some books on Greece and on Socrates. Or just resign myself to the fact that I can't know everything.

"Only Western civilization can be traced back to Ancient Greece," Dad says.

"Will you be able to continue your piano while you're studying Latin?" Mom asks, ignoring Dad's little history lesson.

"Definitely," Link says. "Dr. Koch thinks a relationship exists between my playing by ear and learning a language. He thinks a lot of the time I spent in math was a misuse of certain abilities."

"I see," Dad says.

"I hope Latin will fill your time well," Mom says.

"I will let you know," Link says. In French.

He is still teaching himself Latin when college announcements come through the mail. Last term's grades notwithstanding, Link gets in everywhere he has applied. Even MIT. Dad was right when he said Link tested off the charts. Combined with things like track, which he did because he didn't only want to do math, my brother is an appealing candidate. He gets a full scholarship from the University of Michigan, but the reason Mom and Dad have been killing themselves at work since the day we were born is so that we can each choose a college without financial worry. California doesn't have the allure it once did, Link tells us. Stanford is out. MIT is totally out, since Link does not want to major in math.

"I think Yale," Link says, revealing a packet he has been hiding under his chair.

Mom grabs at the letter and reads it before passing it on to Dad. "He's been accepted, Colin."

"I figured I would get turned down," Link says. "I didn't want to get your hopes up for no reason."

If we could all choose the time we die, there's no doubt in my mind that Dad would choose this moment and exit in perfect bliss.

"Yale," he says. "My God. Yale."

"I understand it's not a bad place to learn languages," Link says.

"Or anything else you might want to study," Dad says.

"Including math," Link says, his voice split down the middle between sarcasm and affection.

Of course we go out to dinner to celebrate. I pull out one of the three unwearable dresses Mom bought for me last fall. Link puts on a tie I recognize as being a gift from James the

Christmas before last. We have reservations at Petrossian, which serves almost nothing but caviar. It's Dad's favorite place in the world, even though Link and I always ask for the pasta special without the sauce, which means we eat plain boiled noodles. Link and I bump up against each other in front of the mirror in the small hallway outside Dad's study. We both do a little preening, and I remind Link that neither of us likes the place we're going to.

"It's not our night," Link says. "This is Dad's victory walk: His son is going to Yale."

"I'll miss you," I say, wondering how in the world I will survive alone with my parents, without the company of the one person in the world who understands them. The one person who knows how to enjoy them when he doesn't want to kill them. The one person whom I used to enjoy most in all the world.

"Sure," Link says. "Just the way you miss me now."

"I do miss you now," I say.

"I can tell," he says. "Yes, you have made that so very obvious. How much you miss me."

Perhaps we are talking about James. Perhaps not. Maybe one day my brother will tell me what he means. I'm not going to drag it out of him. I believe he is smart enough to know I miss him now because of all we have failed to say to each other since the night he called Adena Cohen's father a faggot. I believe that someday, perhaps not until I myself am in college, Link and I will put on nice clothes and go to dinner together.

We will order what we please and enjoy telling each other the secrets of our lives, both past and present. We might talk about James with candor or insight, or he might have become a long-forgotten detail. In another year, that might happen. I can wait. Meanwhile, at Petrossian, I pick around my noodles, scratch at the collar of my dress, and imagine another, better night. A night when I will miss my brother because we have actually been apart. A night during which we have dinner to ensure that we know each other.

It will be long after Link learns Latin and maybe some of that Greek he was threatening to study. I will have to learn a language as well, I am sure. If only the one that my brother uses to articulate his personal unwritten laws. I will learn to care less about knowing who he is and to listen more. I will develop the talents needed for when the opportunity to know him comes my way.

Between now and then, I will do drawings of Link and me alone at a restaurant. During the years before it happens, I will settle for a precise and clear depiction of my imagination. I raise my glass of champagne when Dad does. We all clink glasses and say, "Bravo, much luck, and many more."

Link will go to Yale, he will have his life there, and someday I will know him. You only have to look at my brother's face and see that anything is possible.

CHAPTER TWENTY

J AMES APPLIED TO NONE OF THE COLLEGES HE AND
Link have discussed, which surprises me more than it
should. James now has three places to choose from, and
they are all art schools: the Cranbrook Academy of Art in
Michigan, the School of the Art Institute of Chicago, and
the Academy of Arts in Germany, which is where his
mother went before realizing that money meant more to
her than art.

"You don't speak German," I say, thinking, How on
earth can Mrs. Wentworth have gone to art school? Why
didn't I know this? How come the more I add to the list of
what I know, the list of things I don't know keeps growing?

"I think I'll learn it pretty fast," James says. "It's part of
my requirement in order to pass the first year."

"German is hard," I tell him, picturing Dad terminally
stuck in volume two of *Der Mann ohne Eigenschaften*.

"So is paying for school," James says. "The school in Berlin is free. They have a fellowship program for foreigners. It's why I applied."

"You make it sound like you're going there," I say.

"My father has made it very clear that he will not pay for art school," James says. "And I did not get a scholarship anywhere in the United States."

"Your mother could pay for it," I say. "She'd rather have you in Chicago than in Berlin, wouldn't she?"

"I am not interested in causing a rift between my parents," James says. "I won't tell her there were choices."

I absorb this news in silence. Germany? I can't visit him in Germany. Chicago I could manage and maybe even California, if he'd applied to Stanford, but the idea of James in Europe never occurred to me.

"Your parents want you to have choices," I say. "It's why they sent you to therapy. So that you could choose to be straight or gay."

Choose me. Somebody, please, choose me.

"My father doesn't know I see a shrink," James says. "My mother pays for it. She wants me to have a choice, but she doesn't want me to rub Dad's face in my decisions."

I suddenly realize: James calls his father Dad. And his dad's expectations will shape James the same way my dad's have shaped both Link and me. It's unavoidable. James will go to Germany for reasons that have nothing to do with me, and there will be nothing I can do to prevent it.

"I'm sorry, Ellen."

James sits down next to me on his bed—his bed, where I could never be afraid—and wraps his arms around me, resting his chin on top of my head.

"I'll miss you," I say.

"It will be nothing compared to how I miss you," he says.

When I kiss him, it is to prevent my crying. Especially since I know that if I start, I won't be crying but sobbing. Sobbing the way you do when you're little and your ice cream falls on the sidewalk and it's the end of the world until you get a new one. When he leans into me for the kiss back, his face is wet. He really will miss me. I have indeed been chosen. My brain finally understands what my body has known since Christmas.

I guess what happens now is because neither of us wants to say anything or cry in front of the other. It hurts a little, but not as much as the books say. There's not even a tearing feeling, more a feeling of *oh, how unusual*, until *oh, this is it*. It's nothing like drawing. I don't feel pulled into another place. I am here, finally here. I belong, completely and totally, to this particular beautiful face.

And then it's over. In less than four months I'll turn fifteen, but this will loom larger in my mind, I think.

"I'll always be the first girl," I say.

"Jesus, Ellen," James says, covering his face with his hands.

He is turning red. I have embarrassed him.

"You're super cute," I say, knowing he will hear that I

am *totally madly in love*, Germany or no.

"When's your period due?" he asks, which is not the response I was expecting.

James used a condom, and only as I recall his "Wait, hang on, wait a minute," do I fully think through what having sex can result in: death or pregnancy. Both of them would guarantee I get caught. We were careful, but nothing, as our reading has informed us, is totally effective. And James, whose mother destroyed his father's first marriage when she got pregnant, would have the possibility of pregnancy much on his mind. I am not just the first girl but the first risk for a pregnancy.

"I don't know," I say. "It shows up when it does."

"Start keeping track," he says. "My mother writes it down in a calendar."

When it arrives, if it arrives, my period will carry important information. I picture Mrs. Wentworth some seventeen years ago. She comes slowly into focus as a person. In her closet she could have had a seldom-worn black velvet dress for parties. Certainly a blow dryer in her bathroom, and on her shelves a few books from art school, buried underneath her more important law books.

She wasn't a partner before she married Mr. Wentworth. Just another lawyer working all the time and having an affair with her very married boss. Mrs. Wentworth—Cecily, Celia, what is her name?—flips through her calendar to confirm an appointment (as I have seen my mother do countless times) and notices that something is missing from her schedule. She couldn't have known that Mr. Wentworth would leave his wife for her or that her missed period would become a boy who doesn't want to create a rift between his parents. I see her at her desk, hands over her face. Very scared.

More scared than James and I are now. What will we do if our being careful wasn't totally effective? I think of how things turned out for Mrs. Wentworth. Of how terrified I was the first time James kissed me and how it was the kind of fear I'd walk through again. Anytime. I put my hand on his and say, "Let's pretend we're happy this happened."

"I don't have to pretend," he says. "But don't let anyone after me convince you that this is easily done."

I see a big black hole when I try to imagine having sex with anyone else. But I see a lot of beautiful men and women when I think of James's future lovers.

"You too," I say.

"Yes, yes," he says. "Now let's be happy."

"We went to Petrossian to celebrate Link's getting into Yale," I say. "What would you like to do?"

"I think we've done it," he says, his smile kind of shy, kind of embarrassed, kind of flirting.

My heart gets a vivid and unwelcome preview of what will happen when he leaves for school. James and I, after learning how to navigate our boundaries to become one, will be very separate. We will fade from each other's bodies as we seek new and different company.

"I want you to take my picture to Germany," I say.

"Of course," he says. "I must have a—what is it you say?—a bazillion photos of you."

"No, the drawing," I say. "The one you did of me."

"You're giving it back?"

"I'm loaning it to you," I say. "I want you to remember that girls have interesting qualities."

"I'm not likely to forget that," James says.

"I want you to remember mine in particular," I say.

"That's a given," he says.

"Just say you'll take it."

"Okay," he says. "I will."

"You'll have to do a new one," I say. "One that I can have in its place."

"You want to remember that girls have interesting qualities?"

"Not exactly," I say.

What I want to remember is all the afternoons we spent in hospital cafeterias and airport lounges. How we had full but silent conversations. On lonely days, I'll want to remember that even if no one knows anyone, James made me feel known. And if it happened once, it could happen again. Just like having sex, this time more slowly and deliberately, as if we are memorizing what it was like the first time.

When I reach for my skirt and blouse, it's already past seven. If Mom or Dad is home, I have missed the family dinner hour. The clocks went forward a couple of weeks ago, but I am still disorganized about time and light. I take the twenty dollars James gives me for cab fare because I don't want to argue about safety.

I kiss him at the door and take his whispered "call me" as my due. I walk past the doorman and straight toward Fifth Avenue and Central Park. It is almost May and spring is really here. I intend to go home the way I arrived in October: walking through the park. If I am alone, without my brother's company, then, really, that is how it should be.

During the next several years, I will go on a lot of solo runs through this park. I will find a way to draw what I see. If I never master the art of clear and fearless speech, I will develop clear and fearless eyes. I must. Although I can't imagine them, surely there will be other people besides my brother and James who will give me their attention even as they take all of mine.

After I get out of college or art school, I might run into James at a gallery, as by then I will have learned how to look at paintings without fearing that they are looking back. I'm not clear about where the gallery is, but I know I will be alone. A hand will touch my shoulder and it will be James. Neither of us will have been touched by AIDS or a pregnancy. We won't be particularly enmeshed with anyone else.

It will be the right time for us. And we will know each other again. Or just have a drink to remember that we did. It will be amazing in the way that girl walking through the park is. I see her in her hideous green skirt, acting as if her mind isn't beating with what her body knows. Although I'm still in the process of meeting her, I've already decided to like her.

Not because she's curious, careful, kind, and intense. But because she's let somebody else discover that about her and love her for it.